DARK COMPANY

THE GERMAN LIST

Gert Loschütz, 1946

DARK COMPANY

A Novel in Ten Rainy Nights

Translated by Samuel P. Willcocks

LONDON NEW YORK CALCUTTA

This publication was supported by a
grant from the Goethe-Institut, India

Seagull Books, 2012

First published in 2005 as *Dunkle Gesellschaft. Roman in zehn Regen-
nächten* by Gert Loschütz by Frankfurter Verlagsanstalt
© Schöffling & Co. Verlagsbuchhandlung GmbH,
Frankfurt am Main

First published in English translation by Seagull Books
English Translation © Samuel P. Willcocks, 2012

ISBN-13   978 0 8574 2 085 5

British Library Cataloguing-in-Publication Data
A catalogue record for this book is available from the British Library

Typeset in Sabon LT Standard by Seagull Books, Calcutta, India
Printed and bound by Hyam Enterprises, Calcutta, India

CONTENTS

one

DARK COMPANY

Of course, I had to end up here, having lived my whole life in cities on a river, often on the river itself, with at least one window looking out over the water, having felt all my life that cities without a river hardly even count as towns. Without quite putting it into words, I have always believed that such cities lack a spine, an axis to guide their growth, and that, at most, they only count as a conglomeration of buildings, streets and squares, something more or less haphazardly thrown together with no guiding principle. So, of course, I had to end up in this riverless plain, where the only water we see falls unceasingly from the sky, not as a heavy downpour, rather, a constant dampness, a drizzle, veils and sheets of rain seeping into the soil (also inescapable hereabouts), washing the earth across the asphalted paths that run across the fields, making them into muddy ribbons with an asphalt underlay, a ribbon I follow restlessly at nights when I can't stay in the house, and I know as I walk that at that very moment the boats are passing by all those places where I used to live before.

And how often I used to stand there when the foghorn woke me, stand at the window, the smell of burnt oil hanging in the air, where I could hear the engines putt-putting along and see the yellow misty light that encloses the bridge, the skipper sitting there in the place that should have been mine, on the high stool at the wheel, peering outward at the river where the markers on the banks could hardly be seen in the darkness. That was at night, while in the daytimes the ships of the white fleet would cruise by. Even today, I still know the names of all the tourist ships, *Monbijou*, *Captain Morgan*, *Kehrwieder*, *Condor*, *Ace of Clubs*.

One afternoon, as I was standing there, I noticed a dark company, a group of men and women dressed entirely in black, on the deck of the *Ace of Clubs*. Were they the ones my grandfather had wanted to warn me about? It had been many years ago. On the canal, he showed me the place where his boat used to be tied up, he was wearing his corduroy trousers, and said, 'Beware of the dark company, the ones who never move!' Usually the tourists glance all round, up and down the banks. They turn their heads and nudge one another. D'you see the house there? The bridge? Their voices carry clear across the water. People put their feet up and tilt their faces up to the sun. Young couples hold hands and whisper while their eyes rove the banks, and others stand at the stern and watch the wake washing away to the sides, but there is always movement on the deck, laughter and voices shouting. These people though were sitting on the benches like shop-window dummies, hands in their laps, not a flicker of emotion on their pale faces—their white faces even—their eyes straight ahead and each mouth a thin gash. Even on such a warm day, it seemed that the air there on the sundeck was freezing.

Back when he still sailed, my grandfather had met them on the Thames. He had lost his boat since then, lost it long ago, but the iron rings where he used to tie it up were still there, sunk into the stone slabs overgrown with weeds. He kicked at them with his foot so that they rattled. It was an old canal, a cut linking the Elbe to the Havel, dug back in the middle of the eighteenth century, so we no longer even thought of it as an artificial waterway, rather, as something natural, a real river that just happened not to flow. Slender poplars stood on its banks and a little further up, the willows trailed their twigs in the water. 'The dark ones? Never move?' I didn't know what he meant. 'Leave them be, leave well alone.' He turned round and shoved his hands deeper into his trouser pockets. 'Dangerous people,' I heard him mutter as he walked away, 'Thomas, take care!' And now, so many years later, I saw the ship, the *Ace of Clubs*, glide under the bridge.

Was it the next night? Yes, that was the night when I was woken by a sound, coming from down below, from the river or from the footpath that ran along the bank. A moonlit night, the window was open, and there was the sound again, a whistling or swishing in the air, and when I went to the window I saw the two of them—the woman leaning forward, her hands on the railing, while he was standing behind her. He stood on the footpath and raised his arm, a thin, springy stick in his hand, a switch or a riding crop, he flung his arm out and then brought it whistling down onto her back and her buttocks. Her arms were covered but her dress was lifted up as far as her armpits. The river, and on the other side, the park, the rumbling of traffic in the distance—Spandauer Damm, the ring road, Tegel airport—and down there, among the bushes, the two of them. He lifted his arm the same distance again, a precise movement, measured and then, the switch or riding crop was whistling down. The woman made

a noise, a moan, but did nothing to defend herself from him—
quite the opposite, she told him to keep on. As she loosened
her grip to take hold of the railing more tightly, she turned
her head, looked over her shoulder and nodded. There was a
little light from the bridge, so that I could see her face, the
short nose, the round brow, her hair, gleaming in the moonlight, combed back severely and knotted at the nape of her
neck. He stood with his back to me, lifted his arm again, and
even though a voice inside me was crying out, Stop!, I kept
watching, silent, as though mesmerized, and it was only when
a hand reached out from the shadow of the bushes to give
him a carrying case into which he shoved the switch (or riding crop) that I noticed the others. There they were, the whole
dark company. They were standing in a semicircle, half hidden by the trees and the bushes, and when the two were done,
when he had stowed the switch (or riding crop) and she had
let her dress down again, the group closed round them.

Black suits, black dresses, pale faces, white faces even—
just as he had described them to me as we walked along the
canal. It was after the war. He had been shipping a load of
the bricks made here on the canal and was headed up the
Thames, past the meridian line at Greenwich, he could see
the dome of the observatory on the bank and the towers of
the Naval College where later I would earn my navigator's
licence. He had unloaded at Gray's and then, on the way
back, he ran into a freighter and the barge, which he had
inherited from his father and which he was going to leave to
me, sank within minutes. He was pulled from the water and
taken to the hospital for examination, and as he lay there he
remembered meeting them twice. At the harbour entrance
they had come toward him, on the sundeck of a ferry, that

afternoon, just before they had put in at Gray's, and in the night, he had been woken by a whistling or swishing and, like me, had gone to the window, but wisely enough kept quiet about what he had seen. He never told me.

I leant out of the window and saw them crossing the bridge into town. The next afternoon they would be in another town, sitting on the sundeck of another boat, and the next night they would wake another man with the swishing or whistling switch or riding crop. The moon hung above the park, it was bright as day, but when I turned about I saw that the room was in deep darkness.

The next day two trains collided in the south of Germany, my cat was poisoned by a madman who roamed the riverbank, the shipping company that was considering my application got in touch to tell me that there had recently been a change in the law and that therefore my licence (inshore waters and short crossings, motorized shipping on rivers and coasts) was no longer valid, the stock exchange crashed overnight to its lowest point in years, the bank where I kept all my savings declared itself insolvent and then, a month later, a letter came from my landlord, telling me that he would need the flat back for his own use. This was when I decided to go a long way from any stretch of water, anything even resembling a river, with the result that I think of them all the time. Here, where I ended up, it rains a great deal, the clouds hang low, and when I walk along the mud-smeared asphalt paths at night, I see the cities, the streets where I lived, and I see the rivers, with the ships gliding by.

two

THE NOTE

The rain has become stronger. Tonight when I open the door it slaps me in the face, squalling. I take the umbrella from the basket in the hallway, then put it back again and take my cap from the hook before I go out, through the dripping-wet garden and onto the village green. The street lamps were switched off at the stroke of midnight and since then the green has been in utter darkness, broken by the looming shapes of the rooftops—a farming village hard by what used to be the border, a border still recognizable from its derelict watchtowers spattered with graffiti. Landlocked, the village inn is only open for weddings, christenings and funerals these days, and next to it stands a great boulder left behind by some ancient glacier with a weathered inscription, *Salzwedel, 5 Prussian miles*. The nearest river is the Elbe, a good way away. The core of the village is made up of six farmhouses, only three of them still working today, grouped round the village green. An aerial photograph hanging in the hallway shows that they form a perfect circle, as though drawn with a pair of compasses, an island fringed with oak and beech in the middle of fields that stretch out all round. When I walk the fields at night I hear a murmur, a stamping and snorting which comes, of course, from the byres, built end on to the fields, where the cows jostle and rub, and when I look back through the trees, nearly leafless now, I think I can see the roofline of the cottage I moved into only a month ago, carrying nothing but a suitcase. Ever since my arrival, this feeble rain has been falling, and now that the wind has picked up it becomes more decisive, it carries icy slush along with it, sleet gusting toward me over the fields—sleet, and a sharp wind, just like that night many years ago when I saw Daniel again, on the Ostend crossing.

A sharp north wind drove rain and snow against the ferry as it rolled in the swell, so that as I paced in the salon I could see a blanket of snow slapped over and over again onto the large windows on the luff side and shredded and torn in the wind. Sometimes I was looking at a pane of frosted glass, sometimes through a tattered curtain. Since the heating had stopped working, people kept all their outer layers on, huddled up in wet jackets and overcoats that steamed damply, surrounded by their luggage on chairs and benches that were bolted to the ground. I climbed the stairs and when I came up on the deck I saw a man at the railing in a coat that reached down to his ankles, nipped in at the waist, made of some heavy dark material like naval winter issue, yet at the same time I knew that he was neither a sailor nor a crewman. When the door creaked as it opened, he straightened up and moved off, remarkably light-footed, along the covered walkway, and was still walking like that when he went up on the main decks where the rain and the sleet swept over us. The ship rolling, the wind, the rain, the snow—I braced myself against all this, but he moved as though propelled forward by a hand at his back, holding him under the arms, or as though someone walked in front of him with a great umbrella raised to shelter him from the worst of the weather. The collar of his coat was turned up above his ears, his back toward me, and I could hardly see any more than a tuft of curly hair glittering with rain and snow in the light from the bridge as he passed close by the deckhouse, and as he turned into the other covered way I knew who it was, knew that I knew him, but by the time I turned into the same way he had already gone through a door, into the ship.

And I recall something else. Ostend, the railway station, the waiting room, the table encrusted with food scraps where I wrote to Moorehead after the ferry had come in . . . Mr Henry Moorehead, Royal Naval College, Greenwich . . . *Mister Moorehead, Sir, can it be that Daniel was in London, even though they said that he had gone home?*

At the time, the beginning of the seventies, I lived in a room that was hardly twelve square metres. The door led to a corridor where the duty monitor's whistle would shrill at five o'clock in the morning, a long trilling tone that chased us from our beds, myself and the other cadets and men of the merchant marine who had rooms along the same corridor. The view from my room was of the inner courtyard, a rectangle formed by the main hall of the mansion, its two wings on either side and then the dorm where we lived. If I leant out of the window I could see over the flat roofs of the boathouses beyond the fence, to the blue-grey waters of the Thames.

One wall was almost entirely taken up by a narrow bed with a row of boards, which our predecessors had fished out of the water, cutting them down to the right size and leaving them in the bedframes for us to lie on. None of the beds in any of the dorm's numerous rooms had a mattress or even a slat frame, rather, every one of them had these boards that shoved their sharp edges into our backs and a grey blanket woven with a portrait of a man—according to Griffiths, who lived along the same corridor along with Daniel and Harris, this was the First Sea Lord. On the other wall was a shelf holding the standard reference works of the day and also the books that I would read at night, to transport myself to the banks of other rivers—*Travels to Discover the Source of the Nile*, *The Willows*, *The River*, *Life on the Mississippi* . . . under these was a board fixed to the wall, piled high with the charts and tables that I used to calculate the effect of current on a ship's course and its bearing, and on the door hung an enlarged engraving of Henry Hudson, the explorer I admired above all others for the way he had disappeared. The way he sailed off at dawn (and never returned) spoke to me of true modesty and greatness, unlike the braggadocio of all the other explorers and heroes of the sea.

The light came from a bare bulb hanging from the ceiling. When I lifted my arms getting dressed or undressed, I bumped against it, and if I crossed the room in a hurry I would bump into things, knocking the bedpost, the locker, the board that served as my desk, the doorhandle, and soon enough I had bruises all over. Since my shoulders were broader than the bed itself, I slept on my side and as I went to sleep I could hear the orders of the mate who would send us scrambling into the boats after we woke and whose hoarse shouts sent the boats scudding over the Thames.

He would stand in the stern of the accompanying boat, shouting 'Pull, man, pull!' into his loudhailer while we, cadets and merchant marines, hauled away on the oars. In front of me was the nape of Harris' neck, beaded with sweat, in front of him Griffiths and behind me Daniel gasping and groaning—Daniel, who was due to become First Lord of the Admiralty back in his home country once the examinations were over, a post that was waiting for him. If you asked him about it he would put his hand to his shirt collar as though to check that the button was done up and give a friendly smile without saying a word, so that we decided that there had to be some substance to the rumour. Sometimes he would knock on my door and when I called 'come in,' he would enter and sit on the bed, leaf through my books, look at the poster of Hudson and then leave. In the mess hall he would usually sit at a table on his own, his white uniform shining below the crystal-drop chandelier which cast gleams all about, while his face, brown as tobacco, seemed to melt into the background of oak panels grown dark with the passing centuries. It was as though we could see straight through his face, as though a headless man sat there.

'My God, you can startle a fellow,' I said when he appeared suddenly on the parapet overlooking the Thames.

It was about eleven, eleven o'clock at night, late September, unusually warm. Yes, now that I am braced against the rain and sleet here on the asphalt path, I recall that a warm spell had sent the temperatures soaring. In the afternoon it had been so cold that we were freezing in the maps room, but that evening it was so warm that I had taken off my jacket and laid it next to me. I was sitting on the wall and writing a letter, holding the notepad on my knees with my left hand, pen in my right hand and a torch in my mouth, shining down at the page.

'I startled you? You did me!'

Daniel had been walking along the river and had seen my head floating above the wall like a Halloween pumpkin. 'What are you doing there?' I hesitated, 'Geometry.' In fact, I had been making a note of the incident with the sloop. When we walked on the old towpath it sometimes came over from the Isle of Dogs, sailing slowly toward Deptford Creek, put about and came back toward us, sailed to Lovell's Wharf, turned again and then stopped in midstream. A green light burnt in the wheelhouse, the man at the wheel was nothing more than a shadow. There were curtains at the cabin windows, so that we could not see inside, nor was anyone ever to be seen on the deck, and yet, I had the feeling that someone was looking across at us. The ship lay in the middle of the river, and when we climbed up to the parapet it would come about and go back to the Isle of Dogs.

Daniel came closer and glanced at my pad, so that I put my hand over it. 'Geometry?' He squinted, then turned away and went to the entrance of the tunnel that led through under the dorm to the courtyard, his trousers flapping as he walked. Now it strikes me that he was the only one of us who dressed as though for parade even when he was off duty. We put it down to his family background, for he came from some royal dynasty that the rest of us (the other cadets and the merchant marines) had never heard of but which was still powerful, even today, in East Africa. He turned about at the tunnel mouth—though since his face was once again lost in the darkness I only knew this from the brass buttons on his jacket, gleaming like a beacon chain. Suddenly, the smell of water and diesel from the river was in my nose, and I heard him say in his soft, gurgling voice, 'By the way, Thomas, it doesn't come from the Isle of Dogs.' At that, I stared at the space above the highest beacon. 'Where from, then?' But he had turned round and gone into the tunnel.

This conversation (if you can call it that) took place on the evening of 25 October. I remember this particularly because it was my grandfather's birthday and I wanted to tell him about the sloop. Ever since his wreck, he had collected everything that he could find about the Thames. There were several folders in his cupboard, where he kept his charts, tables, articles and photos. 'Keep an eye on everything!' he had called up to me at the train window when we said our goodbyes. And then I knew that he had made me into his lookout. In this, as I later realized, it was mostly the bad news that caught his interest—columns of smoke above the docks, a Liberian freighter listing to one side as it came down the channel, a Russian sailor pulled dead from the water in the Pool of London. It was these reports that he underlined in red, unlike (for instance) the news I also sent him that the *Queen Mary* had come in, decked to the topmasts with flags and bunting. It was these reports where he put a word or an exclamation mark in the margin.

So it was on the evening of 25 October that I saw Daniel, we exchanged a few words, he made a remark that suggested he could see into my mind, while to me it seemed that his face vanished into the darkness, on 25 October, at about eleven o'clock at night, and never again after that.

The next morning when we climbed into the boats (eights, each with four cadets and four merchant marines) his seat was empty. Instead of him a thin lad appeared above us on the path to the College, another African. At first I thought he was Daniel. It was still dark, or almost dark, not yet light, it was twilight, and just as Daniel had disappeared in the darkness, this lad appeared, accompanied by Speke, the director, who was walking behind him so that I did not see him at once. They came down the path together in the swiftly dawning light. Speke spoke to Allan, the mate, then they came out onto the jetty, Speke, master mariner, and Allan, forty years old, and between them the boy. They towered above him by a head. When they came alongside, Allan squatted and held the gunwale steady while I reached out my hand to the boy. It was a light boat, lying so low in the water that the slightest upset in boarding or leaving was enough to capsize it. I held my hand out to him because I did not want to end up in the Thames, but he hesitated . . . I remember the way he looked at me, somewhat disparagingly, as though unsure whether he could put his hand in mine, and when he did, it felt like grabbing empty air—his hand was like cotton wool—so I grasped his arm a little above the wrist.

Once he was sitting on the sliding seat that until then had been Daniel's place, Allan shoved us off and we rowed over in a few strokes to the buoy that marked the start line, where the other boats were waiting in a group with their oars shipped. And when Allan climbed into the motorboat in which he would follow us, I heard a noise and turned round. The boy was sitting huddled, and his feet in brand-new trainers had slipped from the foot spar and landed with a thump on the bottom of the boat, while his hands sat loosely on the grips. It hardly needs saying that we lost the race by several lengths. Long before the end buoy at Badcock's Wharf, we were so far behind that the others were already rowing back to lap us.

'Where is Daniel?' I asked Allan, after we had drawn the boat from the water. He waved my question aside and then watched the others as they went ahead, Griffiths and Harris taking the shortcut over the lawn while the new boy stayed on the path that led the long way round to the College. Suddenly they veered off course and rushed toward him, both of them good rowers, thickset, sturdy, broad skulls lowered now like battering rams, and I knew that they meant to give him a thrashing for losing them the race (the last before the examinations). But just before they reached the path, he stood still, turned round and looked back at the Thames, at which they faltered, stopped and then veered again, going back to the dorm. And when he raised his hand to shade his eyes, the smooth, easy way in which he moved made me think I saw Daniel again.

At roll call, the navigation teacher, Moorehead, introduced him as Obadja Kwimroe, at which Kwimroe corrected Moorehead and informed him that Kwimroe was pronounced Kwimroi. We were lined up in a horseshoe, with him opposite me so that I had a good view of him. He took one step forward and called out, 'Kwimroi!' His voice echoed through the courtyard, so that all eyes turned toward him. Moorehead was in civvies, wearing his green tweed jacket, the same one I saw later in Griffiths' room—no, not that, not the jacket itself but a scrap of cloth that someone had cut from the lining. In any case, that morning, Moorehead put his hand into his pocket and drew out a sheet of blue paper, a note, glanced at it, then turned to Speke, who otherwise never came to roll call, but this morning the door had been flung open and he came down the stairs and stood next to Moorehead at one of the open ends of the horseshoe. The teacher looked to him but Speke stared past, and Moorehead crumpled the note in his hand and put it back into his pocket. Later, the picture stayed with me, I could summon it up before my eyes—Moorehead's hand with the note (on which the name must have been written, Kwimroe or Kwimroi) and Kwimroe's gaze fixed on it, and when Moorehead crumpled the paper a look of panic showed in Kwimroe's eyes, then, defiance or scorn. Although he was noticeably shorter than Moorehead, all of a sudden, he seemed to be looking down at him, lifting his head a little and looking down at Moorehead, who had already turned away, most likely angry that Speke had not stopped the new boy from breaking school protocol. He went off a little to the side, so that it fell to Speke to tell us, the line already breaking up as he spoke, to announce that Daniel had left college and gone home. I turned round once more in the doorway to the dorm and saw that Moorehead had pulled his spray from his pocket. He stood on the steps to the counting house, holding the little metal bottle to his mouth in one hand and covering it with the other while he pressed the plastic button from below.

Like most of the unmarried teachers, his flat was in the mansion house. Harris had once crept up the stairs and reported that the two rooms were hardly bigger than ours, and crammed full with books. He was a wiry man with a distracted, shuffling walk, an addicted smoker despite the illness that left him gasping for air, and now I can see the yellow–blue packet of Muratti cigarettes shining like a rectangular moon through the sleety rain in the sky above this asphalt track running through fields in Lower Saxony. This was a brand that you couldn't buy in Greenwich, so he brought them from London every time he went. He would go to the city and come back with a clear plastic bag loaded with two yellow–blue tenpacks and numerous green tins of peppermints—we saw him climbing the stairs to the gallery and from there up to his flat. He was always smoking or sucking at a mint and when he felt an attack coming, he pulled out the little bottle and turned aside while he pressed the plastic button with his thumb.

That morning, Kwimroe was wearing the same tracksuit that we all had, the other cadets and merchant marines, but at lunchtime I saw him—like Daniel—in a white parade uniform in the mess, sitting before the dark panels. When I asked whether he knew Daniel, he tugged at his collar as though it were too tight, then smiled and folded his hands on his knee, and his eyes turned to the window. The white of his eyes was shot through with a reddish tinge. When I followed his glance, I saw the Isle of Dogs appear through the rain. The sun had been shining that morning, at noon it had begun to rain, a heavy rain was falling now but at that moment a curtain was drawn aside and then drawn closed once more. 'Daniel,' I said. But Kwimroe was not listening to me, it seemed as though he had quite suddenly dropped off into a deep sleep. Griffiths had followed me to Kwimroe's table and now looked at him sullenly, then raised his head, pulled a face and tapped his forehead with his finger. All at once he gave a start. 'Hey,' he said, 'Come along!' And as we went into the dorm he told me that Daniel had gone home, that he had received a call.

'How do you know that?'

'From Allan.'

'A call?' He nodded.

'When?'

'Last night.'

We had met on the walkway at about eleven o'clock. If he had known at that point that he would be leaving, he would have said something. (Although we were not close friends, we got along quite well.) He would have said, 'Thomas, I'm leaving'. Yet, he had said nothing, meaning that the call had come later. I had looked out of the window at twelve. There was a light burning in the sentry post, the courtyard lay dark, the sky was lit red by the city's glow. It was still very warm, the rain not falling yet but gathering, so that it set a sheen of water on your face. The flag in the middle of the courtyard hung from its pole like a rag. I had closed the window, lay down on the bed and opened a book that Moorehead had given me, *The Great Basin of the Nile*—we had been talking about rivers and their sources. At two o'clock I had turned the light out, so it must have been some-time after that. Sometime after that someone must have come across the courtyard, knocked on his door. 'Mister Kamrasi, telephone!' It was the duty monitor's task, he would climb the stairs and walk along the halls, the click of his boot heels echoing. Even if I had already been asleep by then, I would have woken up, we all would have. But we had not, none of us could remember heels clicking in the hallway or doors opening and closing. Griffiths, who had lived next to Daniel (and now next to Kwimroe), said that he hadn't heard any-thing, as did Harris, whose room was just across the hallway. For some reason I have now forgotten, there was no way to find out the name of the duty monitor. However, I still know that I spoke to Moorehead a couple of days afterwards. The book which he had lent me was by Samuel White Baker. It had been issued in 1886 and had originally been part of the library, then when it had been culled from inventory, because it was in such poor condition, Moorehead claimed it for himself. The binding had been torn off, and I remember that in the chapter on poison arrows someone had written across the pages, *racism*, in red pencil. I returned the book to him and then asked, 'Mr Moorehead, do you perhaps know what happened to Daniel? Why did he go back home?'

It was after class, all the others had already left the room. We were alone. Moorehead looked up, and just as he was beginning to answer, Griffiths put his head round the door and whistled between his teeth, 'Thomas!' At that Moorehead dropped his eyes, looked down at the desk while he gathered his books slowly, put the stack in the middle of the desk and without raising his head, said in a low voice, barely audible, 'Thomas, take care who you spend your time with.' Then he tucked the books under his arm, stood up, went through the other door and out onto the gallery, and suddenly, I remembered something I had overheard that summer. I was sitting on the steps in front of the mansion house, while Moorehead and Speke stood nearby. Moorehead took off his jacket and hung it over his shoulder so that the shimmering yellow-green lining was turned outward, gleaming. As Griffiths and Harris came down the steps, I heard it—'No lights!' Moorehead had spoken softly, more to himself than out loud, it was hardly more than a sigh, but Harris had heard him. He had turned about and glared at him.

'What did you want from him?'

When Moorehead went out, Griffiths came in. He sat down on the desk, leaning on one hand, running the other through his hair while he kept his eyes fixed on me. He looked me in the face, searchingly. He had small grey eyes with short, colourless lashes, his hair shorn down to the standard four millimetres that we all (cadets and merchant marines) wore in these hallowed halls, and for the first time, I saw that his hairline was already receding sharply, male-pattern baldness edging toward the crown of his head. He wore a signet ring on his finger, and sometimes, if he was not making headway with some exercise in class, he would rap out the first few bars of 'With a Little Help from my Friends' on the edge of the desk, drop his hand and then hold it out backwards when he heard my psst, and I would put a note into his fingers.

The short eyelashes, the ring, the searching gaze, the way he sat there on the desk where White Baker and Moorehead's other books had just now lain—I remember now how, all of a sudden, I felt sick of it all, everything I saw, the whole situation, and as though he could read my thoughts (which were hardly thoughts, more a coalescing sense of disgust) he clenched his jaw, thrust out his head until his skull was pointed at me in that battering-ram position, and just when I thought that he would let fly at me (so that I stepped backwards hurriedly) he sagged as though all hope were lost to him. 'Oh, Thomas!' He nodded twice, as if to concede some point I had made, and as he did so, I heard a faint whistling as though from a punctured lung. Then he hoisted himself down from the desk and took my arm in a sudden access of affability. When we went out into the gallery, Harris and Kwimroe were standing there, though I had never seen the two of them together before, Harris leaning on the wall next to the stairs that led up to Moorehead's flat, Kwimroe across from him, leaning on the balustrade. Although they tried to act as though they were standing there quite by chance, they had clearly been waiting for us.

Harris winked at me, and I recalled the yellow–blue packet of cigarettes that he had brought from Moorehead's flat as proof that he had really been there, sharing them between us—himself, Griffiths and me. I stepped up onto the stairway, without quite meaning to, and looked up, where Harris had crept in, and even today, I remember how the treads of the wooden stair sagged in the middle like a rope held slack, and remember Harris' voice behind me at the same time.

'If you're looking for him, he just went past.'

A couple of weeks later, we—Griffiths, Harris, Kwimroe and myself—were walking along the towpath, I bent to pick up a stone, flicked my wrist and sent it skipping across the water. A bright day, mid-November, the trees on Island Gardens shining across like rows of red-and-yellow beacons. Harris and Griffiths had already begun to chum up with Kwimroe, I might almost say that they had become inseparable. They would sit at his table in the mess hall, and when I went along the corridor at night I heard their voices behind his door. In the classroom they would pull their desk backwards a little so that they could see him without having to turn their heads. (They sat bolt upright, eyes front, but I could see that their bodies were turned just a tiny bit toward him, as though waiting for some command.) I hung back slightly and looked across to the Isle of Dogs, and when I turned round, I noticed Kwimroe's eyes, he looked at me searchingly, the black pupils ringed by their brown iris, floating in those red-and-white eyes. Harris and Griffiths had gone ahead a little, they bent down, picked something up, and when Kwimroe nodded to me as if to say that I should join them, I turned round and went back. From the parapet I could see Harris and Griffiths standing there with him. Kwimroe showed them something, he lifted his arm and something lay on his open palm. I squinted, but was too far away to make anything out. The two of them bent forward, then straightened up and looked over to the parapet. Standing in the same spot where I had sat the night when Daniel appeared out of the darkness, I took a step backwards and went into the tunnel.

When I knocked on Griffiths' door that evening, he was lying on the bed staring at the ceiling. A bottle with a milky fluid stood on the windowsill, wound about with thin strips of leather, glass beads, nails and shards of various sizes and colours, all of which made up a pattern of interlocking rings, and between these was a strip of paper like the note that Moorehead had taken from his pocket at roll call, a thin blue strip on which Griffiths had written MOOREHEAD in large letters. 'Griffiths,' I said, 'are you worried you'll forget the name? Or what's this supposed to be?' But he did not answer, simply lay there staring at the ceiling, and when I went to Harris, across the hallway and one door down, I found his door locked.

That night—the night before the first written examinations—I kept waking up. The window was open, the wind was blowing in. I shut it but the wind pounded against the panes in furious gusts, the glass rattled, papers were blown off the board that was my desk and they scurried into every corner of the room, and the poster of Hudson was torn where the wind had flapped at it—it was only held onto the door by drawing pins. The wire cable on the flagpole clacked outside in the courtyard, the lightbulb swung back and forth and about three o'clock—I looked at my watch—the wind prised up the rooftiles and a howling sound moaned through the hallways, which were utterly deserted when I looked out of my door. When I looked in the mirror in the morning, I saw that the sharp edges of those hand-me-down bedboards had left deeper marks than usual (probably because the blanket had slipped), red welts slanting across my shoulder and arm. When we sat for our exams that morning, each at our own desk, spaced out widely in the maps room, they throbbed painfully and persistently.

The examination began at nine o'clock sharp, and when Moorehead gave the order to collect the papers at three, the throb had given way to a cramping numbness, so that I had trouble lifting my arm. When I met Griffiths in the doorway I shoved him aside and ran to the dorm to look at my shoulder. I can still remember how I was standing there half-naked in front of the mirror when Griffiths came in and asked whether he could help, and I replied, 'What with, Griffiths?' And I remember that when he lifted his hand and pointed to my shoulder—'My God, what is that?' although nothing could be seen but a little discolouration—I noticed that he had swapped his signet for another ring, made of wire or steel, that could have been bent from one of the thin nails that had been lying on his windowsill. When he saw me looking at it, he dropped his hand and asked if I wanted to come along.

'Where to?'

'Walk along the Thames for a bit.'

'Good,' I said, 'I'll come.' Not because I wanted to at all, but rather because I did not want him to think that I was avoiding them because they had joined forces with Kwimroe. I wanted as well to ask him what the previous evening's performance had been. Have you taken up sleeping with your eyes open, too? He went out into the hall to wait for me. I got dressed, and as I followed I saw him and Harris sitting on the steps, while Kwimroe leant against the window frame on the landing below. He was wearing a thick grey coat which made him look more grown up than usual, but when he raised his head I saw the same childlike face that I had remarked in Daniel, a perfectly smooth, unlined face with not the faintest sign of a beard.

He walked ahead of us, arms still folded, on the way down to the quay where we usually joined the towpath, and although he was too far away to hear me, I didn't ask what I wanted to ask, not about sleeping with his eyes open, and not about the object on the windowsill either, which I associated with Kwimroe without knowing why.

I walked between Griffiths and Harris, both of them silent, all three of us silent, and when they hurried ahead to catch up with Kwimroe, I hung back, then turned aside, took King William Walk instead and went through the foot tunnel beneath the Thames that leads to the Isle of Dogs, which lay ahead of us in the evening haze. I came out of the tunnel behind Island Gardens and went down Saunders Street to Newcastle Drawdock, where the sloop used to put in after turning about. I had not seen it for weeks now. Apart from a few converted fishing boats that were now used as yachts, already covered with tarpaulin for the winter, there was only a lightship there, streaked white with gull droppings, its bridge windows smashed and shattered. It had become quite dark by now. Across the Thames and a little way over, the towers of the Naval College and directly opposite me, Lovell's Wharf thrusting out into the river, where I thought I recognized the silhouettes—the lights were just coming on—of Griffiths, Harris and Kwimroe, looking across from the other side.

That was at the beginning of December, the first day of examinations and the last time when I spoke to them—that's to say, until the afternoon of the day we all went home, when all the doors of the dorm were open. The examinations stretched out over three weeks, a time which has remained with me as a bad memory. I went to bed early, fell asleep early, woke up early, memorized everything that was on the curriculum, and as I went into the maps room everything was in my head, but when I tried to lay hands on it, I seemed to hear a wind whirring toward me and all that I knew ended up like the papers, blown off the board desk, that had scurried into every corner of the room, just as I had crawled about on the floor that night to recover them, now (with time running out on me) I scrambled in every corner of my mind for the facts scattered there. I looked round, desperate, and when I thought I had found them and began to write, I realized that they were the wrong ones, had nothing to do with the question, useless, and I began to look hither and yon in the maps room, as though the facts could be found somewhere outside me, and noticed that Griffiths and Harris (usually hither-and-yon men themselves) were filling page after page at the same pace as Kwimroe, who sat to their right. And since I did no better in the oral examinations, it was probably only thanks to Moorehead's intervention that I passed after all.

For the graduation ceremony we sat in Burton Hall, which was otherwise only opened for lectures by politicians. Because Christmas was coming, it had been decked out with pine branches and mistletoe, giving an almost cheerful look to the cold hall, which looked like a nave. We waited, straight as ramrods, legs at an angle of ninety degrees to our body, our forearms set (as protocol dictated) thirty centimetres apart like two lengths of wood on the desks in front of us, waiting to be called individually to the rostrum. When my turn came, Speke looked straight past me, and his handshake when he congratulated me was as limp as Kwimroe's had been when I had helped him into the boat. As I went back down the centre aisle he was coming toward me, a small, slight figure against the dark wall at the back of the hall, and when our paths met he raised his head and lifted his eyelids in the same way he had looked down on Moorehead that morning at roll call, gazing with those eyes, always a little red, and then the next moment he had gone past. And as I took my place, I heard Speke's words, heard that—*Mr Moorehead, Sir, how is that possible?*—he, Griffiths and Harris, in that order, had scored the top marks in that year's examinations.

After the ceremony I went through the tunnel and walked down to the Thames.

'Thomas!'

I turned round. It was Moorehead. He had come after me, I saw his head above the parapet. As I climbed the steps, he came toward me, took my arm and gave it a squeeze as he said, 'Thomas, is there anything you want to tell me?' But I did not know what, or how, and if there was, how I could begin without sounding as though I were making excuses. So, I simply shook my head. And when he climbed back up the steps, the smell of salt and diesel was in my nose, just as it had been on the day I last saw Daniel. *Mr Moorehead, Sir, it is only now, here in Ostend, that I think I should at least have told you what I had seen a couple of hours before.*

Before I went into Burton Hall, I had looked in on Griffiths to say goodbye, even if we were no longer friends. The door was open, all the doors were open and people were hurrying to and fro between the rooms. Most of them were leaving that day, so they were busy packing, meeting the others one last time and exchanging addresses. My train left at 22.15 from Victoria Station and since I did not know whether I would see Griffiths and Harris after the ceremony I looked round the door, but Griffiths' room was empty, he had gone out. There was a scrap of cloth lying on the bed which I recognized straightaway as the shimmering yellow-green lining of Moorehead's jacket. And as I was still wondering what this could mean, he came in with Harris and said that I should hold this, pressing into my hand a root with five forked growths that made it—head, arms, legs—look like a puppet, took the piece of cloth, wrapped the root up in it and then while I was still holding it, tied it tight with the leather strips from the windowsill, as though he were tying up a piece of meat for the roast. He tugged the strips so tight that the cloth bulged up in places round them, after which—'Wait, Thomas!'—he went to the windowsill and took a note from a book lying there, a strip of white paper as long as my thumb, which he pierced with a nail and then stuck into the mannikin root, wrapped up in that scrap of Moorehead's jacket lining and bound about with strips of leather. It was as though he were putting an address on a parcel, and indeed, there was a word written in ink on the other side, a few letters or loops and curlicues showing through the paper, and by the time I had pieced them together into Moorehead's signature (it must have been cut from an exercise book) Harris had taken the package away from me, while Griffiths clapped his meaty hand—'Thanks!'—on my shoulder. *Mr Moorehead, Sir, this is what I should have told you*. But I confess that I had thought the whole thing was one of those pranks played at examination time and graduation, admittedly coarse but quite customary. And how could I have explained being an accessory?

That evening though, Moorehead had hardly gone back through the tunnel when I saw what I would have to call a procession on the path down to the quayside, Kwimroe at its head, goose-stepping toward the Thames. Kwimroe, then Griffiths, then Harris. It was dark but as they passed the light burning above the door to the boathouse I saw that Harris was holding the parcel which I had helped to wrap, carrying it before him with such a sense of ceremony that I thought again that it was a hoax, a leg-pull, a piece of theatre or mummery. But for whose benefit? There was no one there to applaud them. They walked out onto the wooden jetty, which creaked beneath their feet, Griffiths turned round, in his hand two stones that he had been carrying close to his body, and now that the three of them were gathered at the edge of the jetty he strapped the stones to the package with a belt, to the puppet, the root, the thing wrapped up in lining from Moorehead's jacket, the thing labelled with his name, that was addressed to him or meant to represent him, then handed it on to Kwimroe, who bowed slightly as he took it. He squatted down and sank it into the river so gently that from where I stood nothing could be heard but a gurgle, like air bubbling from the neck of a bottle. I had followed them diagonally across the grass and as they turned onto the towpath, three abreast, headed for Lovell's Wharf, I ran to the dorm. Not half an hour later, I went to the railway station, catching the ferry two hours after that. *Mr Moorehead, Sir, I would be more at ease if you could write me a few words. As mentioned, I am in Ostend. Hoping that I have not made a mistake—*

By then it was nearly morning, and since I wanted to send the letter straightaway, since there was no time to lose, I went out onto the streets, but the post office which I eventually found was—of course—closed. A hotel, I needed a hotel, perhaps they would have a stamp . . . and just as I saw the neon sign proclaiming 'Imperial', a large car came up the street toward me from the port, drove slowly past, stopped, and the interior, light came on, the driver bent over a map as though looking which way to go. He was wearing a peaked cap, while a dark-skinned man sat in the back seat, the collar of his coat turned up. I headed for the car, then turned and went into the Imperial, where a sleepy-looking girl sold me a stamp when I showed her the letter, taking it from a black folder which also held photographs of copulating couples which must have been taken by cameras placed in the rooms. The photographs were kept in plastic sleeves marked with Roman numerals, and when she saw me looking at them across the counter, she asked, 'Do you want one?' But although I liked the photos, I was too shy to say yes. She gave me a friendly glance while I stuck the stamp onto the envelope. As I left, she walked me to the door. The car had driven off. The sleet had reached Ostend. We could hear the metallic thunder of the loading hatches closing down in the harbour.

Years later, I met Allan on the street by chance. He didn't recognize me, but once I introduced myself he told me that Moorehead had been found dead on the stairs to his flat that same evening, head down, the spray in his hand; that after the Falklands War, Griffiths had been promoted to be the youngest admiral in the Royal Navy and that Harris had recently been appointed undersecretary in the Department of Trade and Industry. I was only in London for two days. We were standing on the corner of Portobello and Lonsdale Road, less than two minutes from my hotel, with scraps and snips of paper fluttering all round us as a boy threw them from a window above a costermonger's stall, and as we said goodbye—Allan shook my hand—I realized that he had confused me for someone named Bruce. 'Mr Bruce,' he said. Mr Bruce. And now the pictures that I saw the next day also flimmer into life against the sleet, here on the asphalt path, pictures on the television screen in the hotel lobby—I had just paid—from the BBC news, the United Nations, a black man speaking at the podium, peering at his manuscript, and as I took my suitcase someone leant into the image from behind, handed him a note, straightened up again—and although the whole thing had taken no more than a second, although he was not in the picture for longer than a second, I am sure that it was Kwimroe I saw.

three

ON THE NIGHT TRAINS

It has hardly rained at all for a few days now, though to compensate, the wind has become stronger, sweeping across the fields where the snow has long melted, sending up little sprays of water, finding its way into the house through the cracks to tear the handle from your hand and send the doors slamming. The wind moans in the chimney, rattles the windows, and when I go out at night I can hear a shrill whistling. Is it from the windmills up on the hill, slicing the air to pieces with their blades? A whistling, rushing sound, and beneath it, as though from a long way off, a clicking and clacking like the sound of the cable beating against the flagpole in the courtyard of the Naval College. Not to forget the clinking—is it from the tinfoil strips on the cherry trees in the orchards? Or is it rather from the coins that sat in my pocket in the old days, back on the night trains? Tips that the passengers had given me.

These people are afraid of flying, I would think when I saw them coming onto the platform in the evenings with their suitcases. Why else, when for the same price they could reach their destination in a fraction of the time by aeroplane, would they submit to being freighted across Europe by night, crammed into a narrow berth? By the time I welcomed them aboard at the carriage door, I had already made up the folding beds so as not to have to do it before their eyes, I had put the sheets onto their thin mattresses and drawn up the bed-clothes. 'Can I bring you anything?' I would ask when I knocked on their doors a little while later. Yes, most often I could, a nightcap, a little drink against the unaccustomed excitement of the journey. We could offer a little bottle of whisky, the size of your thumb, which I would serve on a tray, with ice from the cool box if so desired. Or a cognac? A schnapps? A quarter litre of Merlot in a plastic cup, from a screw-top bottle? As they paid they would round up the price—that's fine, thank you—or dig out some coins and drop them into my pocket. Italian lira, French francs, Swiss francs, Danish kroner, and when I was back in Berlin I would chuck them all in a jar on a shelf by the door in my flat and, every now and again, would take them down to the bank to change for Deutschmarks. At the time—that was the mid-eighties—the view from my window, between two buildings, was of the Havel, where the barges shoved their bow-waves along before them while the trains came and went on the rail-way bridge above the river, also in view, and for a moment train and ship would meet before going their separate ways once more.

My shift began late in the afternoon, or early in the evening, when I went to the office to get the docket for the sleeping car. There is not a great deal to be said about the work itself other than that we needed to be able to live and work in the hours of darkness, to do mental arithmetic and to remain courteous. The job also needed a fair few books, read and replaced, to help pass the time between midnight and the morning. When I wrote as much to my grandfather, he wrote back saying, 'Then you might just as well have signed on to one of those tin cans which lurk under the pack ice for half a year at a time, never surfacing, breathing compressed air, eavesdropping.'

As soon as I heard the clacking of the doors being bolted, I would walk the length of the train, through the other compartments, looking at the people slumped in their seats, and when I saw a book I knew lying in an otherwise empty compartment, I would sit by the window to await the return of the owner. Once he had taken his place I would look at his reflection in the window, hoping to learn something about myself by watching him, as though those who read the same books are members of one family, their resemblance showing not in the faces or in the build but in a particular way of holding oneself, that I hoped to discover in the reader and thus in myself as well. Is that how I looked? Did I have that same assured gaze? Or had these journeys begun to change me?

As time went by, the world outside vanished. The fields, the meadows, the ditches, the ranks of trees and the forested slopes or bare cliffs loomed up suddenly beside the line, the bridges and tunnels, the suburbs with their factories, warehouses, car parks or fairgrounds—all of this became simply scenery, a painted flat wound past the window, as unreal as the lodgings that all looked alike, the hotels with stacks of tatty newspapers on the lobby tables, narrow stairs leading up to rooms with bright chequered wallpaper, cell-like rooms for a bed only, all furnished alike—the luggage rack by the door, the fitted wardrobe, the bed, the television in the corner. The windows either did not shut properly, so that travellers were always on the brink of catching cold, had earache, a sore throat or they could not be opened at all, so that hardly had I fallen asleep than I woke up again, the air gone, and lay awake, lying on my back, and listened to the knocking of the pipes, where someone hammered away steadily as though hacking at rust with a chipping hammer, the rhythm of his strokes matching the rhythm of the questions that chased one another through my head. What now? Where next? I had just turned thirty-five and had lost my barge to the wreckers' yard—it belonged to a loss-making company—and the next day (out of spite? a mania for independence? a wild urge to be free of the shipping firms, the dispatchers which had taken over from the old owner captains) had made my way to the recruiting offices of the sleeping car company. What now? Where next? tapped the man with the hammer, sitting somewhere in the pipes. Not forgetting the bathrooms, gloomy place tiled to the ceiling, mostly with a shower cabin that had been squeezed in later, so narrow that if you dropped the soap and wanted to pick it up you would have to step out of the cabin, where it was impossible even to bend. We learnt the paths from lodgings to railway station, from office to train, from train to office, from station to lodgings, could have walked them with our eyes shut, though in summer the sun was in our eyes, either just rising or just setting. In winter it was still dark as we walked or dark once more. And in between, the clacking of the wheels, the subdued light in the train corridors, the scenery of country or town winding past the window, scenery which only stopped for a moment at stations—all this made the world outside (although we were outside, of course) dissolve into a fuzzy stroboscopic fog of impressions.

Some of my colleagues, the older ones, had not been home for more than a year, it was a moot point whether they still had homes, whether they didn't live in the trains by now, which is why they reminded me of that particular sort of homeless folk who live in the New York subway tunnels, never coming up to daylight, who stayed in my mind most lastingly from the one time that I was there. Shadow people, whose skin had without exception taken on an olive-green tint, regardless of whether it had originally been black or white. Some of them had eyes sunken deep into their sockets, while others had protuberant eyes that sat in their faces like little knobs, either mole eyes or frog eyes which they could turn in all directions without moving their head. Instead of taking the lifts, which would have hurled me upwards as fast as a motorcar drive, to take a look at Manhattan, I returned over and over again to these Stygian scenes, riding the subway here and there, not knowing where I was going. Sometimes, then, the rattling of the train would explode into a hellish noise and looking up you would see a green-skinned figure take his place in the doorway between cars. He had come through from the next car and hesitated a moment before coming down to the middle of this one, singing, dancing, often with absurd contortions, telling his tale of woe. Some had one story, others another. And for all of them the story always ended the same way. For all of them, the subway tanned their faces with its own dirty tint, an olive-green that you could see, when you looked for it, in my colleagues' faces too.

The nights spent on the train had burrowed into their faces—their foreheads were lined, their eyes wavered, deep furrows ran from the nostrils to the corners of their mouth. When they left the train they would stumble like sailors getting used to dry land under their feet again. You knew by the way they carried their suitcases that there was less and less inside from one journey to the next, until at last (so I imagined) they carried only their uniforms and toothbrushes, everything else having been scattered to the winds. Their personal effects, letters, photographs, mementos had long ago been left behind somewhere, or stolen, and when you heard them speak it was as though at the same time they had lost their memory or the will to remember.

The stories they told were either of things that had happened long ago or of recent events, tales of evenings in bars or trouble with women, but never anything about the time in their life immediately before they joined the sleeping cars. They would edit out this period or break off in the middle of a sentence if they caught themselves mentioning it by chance. When I listened to them, their voices were always too loud, as though even here in the hotel room they still had to drown out the noise of the train, and suddenly, I began to realize that they hadn't just lost their sense of balance, that something else was out of kilter too, and whatever this was, they were hiding it deep within themselves. They would begin to talk, fall silent, turn to the wall and pull the bedclothes up round their ears.

Rome, Via Principe Amadeo, not two hundred metres from the station, early June, humid and warm. I had opened the door to the hallway to let a breeze through, to no avail, the air stood in the middle of the room like a heat-soaked block of marble. Through the wall I could hear the cards players smashing their hands down onto the table, and at every crash the block of stone seemed to grow and to give out a few more degrees of heat. After a while I got up and went to the shower at the end of the hallway to fetch the shirt that I had washed and hung on a wire hanger, over the metal frame of the shower cabin, but it no longer hung there. Someone (one of the cards players whose hands I could still hear crashing onto the table, stoking the heat?) had taken it (to make room for his own shirts?), held it out of the window and let go. I saw it lying on a ledge on the facade of the house next door and when I spotted it I grabbed the two shirts that were hanging there instead of mine, tore them down from the rail and sent them flying where mine had gone. They were still damp, flapped against the facade as they fell, peeled away again and fell to the street, where a car snagged hold of them and dragged them off.

'That wasn't fair,' said a colleague (he was actually one of the cards players, a group which rode a different route), as we—the cards party, myself and Wilhelm, my colleague in the sleeping car—went to the station through the heat of the evening, almost worse than the heat of the day, *two for one*, conceding that in principle he understood what I had done, while Wilhelm worked his lower jaw back and forth, as was his habit, so that we could hear a faint cracking sound. He was the oldest there. His hair had originally been blond but was now thinned to grey strands which he would plaster across his pate. The skin of his scalp had that olive-green tinge. He was already wearing the white shirt and red waistcoat, while the rest of us were still in mufti, light summer trousers that were still too hot in this heat and short-sleeved shirts. The suitcase swung loose in his hand and suddenly, I knew that he carried nothing in it but his tie. Regulations required we tie the thin grey strip so that the emblem with the three letters of the sleeping car company showed a hand's-breadth below the knot.

Was that the night when he came out of his car and joined me at the window? The huddled lights of small towns flew past, while a storm flickered over the mountains, we could briefly see a river winding past (the Ticino?). He smoked. When he puffed on the cigarette the glow lit his face up in the window. He told me that his wrists hurt, his legs, his back. And suddenly he said, as though fed up with his complaints and looking for a new topic to talk about, that he could have prevented the Second World War, the murder of the Jews, Teheran. Yalta, the Potsdam Agreement, the division of Europe, the Berlin wall, perhaps even the Vietnam War and a number of smaller wars (though he couldn't remember, he said, how those other wars broke out, how they ran their course or the outcomes).

'Really?'

'Yes.'

He nodded. It had been in Dresden, at the end of the Thirties, he was a young hotel page at the time and he had been instructed to push the breakfast trolley into a particular room, the best in the hotel, not actually a room as such, rather a suite, no, a whole floor that was separate from all the other floors. He had been picked for the task from among all the other pages (twelve in all, whose duties were otherwise to open and close doors, press the buttons in the lifts or bow as they handed over messages). The directors of the hotel were walking in front of him, beside him and behind him, one of them knocked on the door, someone opened, he pushed the cart into the room bearing its mushroom omelette, toast, a fruit bowl, a teapot over a little spirit stove, the plates and cups and cutlery, and when he looked up he saw Hitler sitting on the edge of the bed in gown and slippers.

'All I would have needed to do was take one of the knives from the trolley and shove it into his throat.'

His cigarette, his third, glowed once more and his face in the window lit up darkly. 'Yes,' I said, 'that's a good story.' And then I asked the inevitable question, 'Would you have?'

'What?'

'Stabbed him?'

At which, instead of answering he lifted his arm and wiped the window, turned round and shuffled off to the sleeping car, cracking his jaw. It was about two o'clock in the morning, still very warm but, of course, nothing in comparison to the afternoon heat in the Via Principe Amadeo, where a few days later he was picked up from the hotel. Lipski, one of the cards party, met him on the steps as he came back from an errand. Wilhelm between two men whose appearance Lipski could not recall when I asked him later for a description.

Lipski was a short, spindly man with deep-set eyes, always with faint dark bags below them, whose skin was still astonishingly light in tone but stretched over the bones of his face like parchment. He had come back into the dark stairway after the shimmering noon heat on the Principe Amadeo and was almost blind for a moment, so that it was only by the skin of his teeth that he missed colliding with one of the two men, who were even wearing dark suits. He would have walked straight into them if he had not heard a hissing, an exhalation, and stood with his back pressed to the wall to let them by, since none of the three made any attempt to move aside. Wilhelm had not looked at him, instead staring dead ahead and simply shoving his jaw from side to side.

In the evening we walked to the station again, Lipski with his colleagues, while Wilhelm, who usually walked at my side, was not there. Lipski reckoned that he might already be waiting on the platform, but he was wrong about this, so that I had to take over his car as well, helped by the conductor.

The conductor greeted the guests at the gate and led them to their compartments, collected their tickets and passports and put them into a briefcase that he handed to me so that I could see to all formalities at the borders without having to wake them. At around two o'clock I was just about to set out on my rounds when the train stopped in the middle of nowhere, I looked out and was startled, thinking that I saw Wilhelm running over the railway embankment and disappearing between the bushes, into the darkness. The conductor went up to the engine to find out why we had stopped and when he came back he reported that the locomotive had stopped for no (perceptible) reason, that no, the emergency cord had not been pulled, the instruments would have showed us if it had been. He was about my age but taller and fatter, so that when he went along the corridor he almost filled its whole height and width. When the train set off again he looked at his watch, took a notebook from his pocket and noted down the time, two twenty-three, then entered 'halted from—to—' in his logbook under 'Unusual incidents', which mattered to the extent that it allowed us to compare the time of our stop with that of other trains. The facts were that that night, all trains travelling anywhere north of Rome had stopped as though by agreement (or obedient to a secret order)—at three minutes past two the engines stopped, the wheels locked up, the trains came to a halt and could only be induced to move once more, despite the best efforts of the engine drivers, at two twenty-three. During these twenty minutes, all rail transport north of Rome came to a full stop while southern regions reported nothing more than minor faults.

It was a few days after that, on an afternoon as hot and bright as when Lipski had seen Wilhelm on the stairs between the dark-clad figures, that I heard a knock on my door in the Principe Amadeo. I called for whoever it was to come in. Two men entered, showed me their accreditation as members of the criminal investigation department and asked me to come with them to the Forensic Institute on Porta Pia for an unpleasant task—I was to help identify a man who might be my missing colleague. This told me that when I put in a report on the basis of Lipski's remarks, the sleeping car company had passed it on to the police. One of the two men spoke German. When I asked, he said that the unidentified man had been discovered by the cleaning crew on the metro, sitting at a window as though asleep, at the final station, Ostia Lido. The ticket in his pocket had been validated at Piramide station at four o'clock in the evening. Since time of death was estimated at around five in the evening, it seemed that he had shuttled back and forth between Rome and Ostia until the service stopped running (zero hours seventeen).

They helped me into a car, which however refused to start, so we got out and walked, since they could not agree on whether to take a bus or taxi, first along the Via Cavour, then, once we had passed the station, through several smaller streets, the last of these leading not to Porta Pia but to the Viale del Policlinico. The sun was directly overhead, the streets lay as though deserted, the blinds had been let down on all the houses, a cat lay curled up inside a tyre, and suddenly I thought that if *I* should happen to disappear next, then the cat would be the only one to have seen me in their company. The cat raised its head idly. And suddenly I thought of a distinction which my grandfather liked to draw, that in the south—because streets and squares lay deserted in the noon heat—midday was a favourite time for kidnappings and murders, while we in the north preferred to take care of such business at night.

Since their argument over bus or taxi the two of them had fallen silent. The younger one, who walked on my left, was wearing brown sandals, in which his toes stuck out a little over the edge of the sole, so that every time he took a step it seemed that the toes on his back foot touched the paving stones. The other was wearing heavy black shoes which obviously had tacks on the soles, for their clacking echoed along the street. Neither of them however was dressed in dark clothes. The younger one wore light-coloured trousers and a green–red–blue safari shirt with an open collar, the other was dressed entirely in beige, or khaki, his shirt likewise open, with a thin silver chain about his neck, which bounced against the grey hair of his chest as though against a trampoline with every step. It was this second man who knocked on the iron door of the clinic's basement and turned the handle once we heard '*Si, avanti*'. We entered a large room, tiled lime green right up to the ceiling, icy cold after the heat outside. I had been expecting to see one of those steel refrigeration cabinets that fill up the whole wall, familiar from the films but, instead, there were a number of tables standing in the middle of the room, covered with sheets, the contours of bodies visible beneath them. Circular neon tubes hung from the ceiling, giving off a light that was like fog or even gauze, so thick that it seemed you could cut it with a knife. A man got up from his swivel chair and came across to us. He was wearing a grey coat and stood at the table in the middle, then removed the sheet so that I could get a look at the face. The dead man's eyes were closed, his nose was sharp, the mouth just a line, and in the foggy or gauzy light the whole face was waxy, forbidding. The lower jaw was held shut though, with a strip of fabric that ran up round the top of the head. This was what confused me so much for a moment that I saw Wilhelm, saw him pushing his jaw to and fro and heard the cracking sound, so that even when I was back out on the street I wondered whether it might not have been him after all. But it was not, I am sure of that.

This is what I told Lipski as well. When I went into his room, he was sitting at the table and staring at the cards stacked up in four piles in front of him. They were smaller than an ordinary deck of cards and there were more of them than most games need. They formed a row of four little towers, but as I came in he knocked his hand against them, they collapsed and he began to sweep them round the tabletop with circular motions of his hands. He was completely naked and I saw that there was no hair at all on his body, not a whisker anywhere. Though I remembered his parchment-like skin as quite pale, it had darkened, taut over the shoulders and at the ribs, and his penis, lying between his legs, was like a young child's. When he noticed where I was looking he picked up a handkerchief and placed it over his lap.

'Lipski,' I said. 'I've just come from the morgue.' But he seemed not to be listening, simply looked at the window. The blind had been let down halfway and the light that entered lay in white stripes across his face. He sat there completely motionless, chin thrust forward, arms hanging down. He only raised his hands once I left and began to mix and shuffle the cards again. But he had understood what I had told him, for as we were on our way to the station that evening, he remarked, 'I could have told you that straightaway.'

'What?'

'That he's not there where they took you.'

'And how did you know?'

He rocked his head from side to side, just as Wilhelm used to, and stopped in his tracks the next moment when he realized what he was doing. He froze and his deep-set eyes seemed to start forward a little. We were in the middle of the Via Carlo Cattaneo, just crossing to turn into the Via Giovanni Giolitti that ran along the southern side of the station, the evening traffic streamed about us, cars, horns honking, headlights flickering on and off. 'Lipski, what is it?' His chin was trembling. But he simply shook his head and didn't say another word.

These are the facts—Wilhelm was fetched from the hotel in the Principe Amadeo by two men dressed in dark clothes at midday and has been missing ever since.

I described what had happened to my grandfather, who wrote back saying that he believed that all those who had vanished had not really vanished at all but were all gathered somewhere, in designated places. If I have understood correctly what he was saying, they travel in a particular kind of train which carries them across the length and breadth of Europe, unceasingly; that is to say, they never leave the train. He told me that every one of these people has his own compartment in which to sit and read or simply stare out of the window. Since these trains are not listed on any timetable and never stop—or stop only in very remote, hidden places—it is difficult to detect them. Later, he expanded upon his theory.

It was certainly possible, he wrote in another letter, that the missing people were also housed in the dilapidated high-rises at the edges of cities, where they form their own colonies, cut off from the rest of the world.

I got back to Berlin the next evening, the evening after my visit to the morgue and after an uneventful journey during which Lipski sat silently in my compartment, as though afraid to be on his own. 'Lipski,' I had asked, 'What is it? Is something bothering you?' but he kept quiet and the only sound was the riffle of the cards as he slid them from one hand to the other. When I got back that evening I dropped the coins into the jar by the door and when I went to the window I saw the Havel flowing backwards between the buildings, an effect doubtless produced by the wind blowing against the river's flow.

four

THE GARDEN

No wind now, the wind has died down but instead fog, silence and the smell that so often accompanies fog, a smell of fire, a burning smell, a hint of smouldering trees and smoke creeping over the ground at knee height, a smell like that in the garden near the small town where I was driven at night thirteen years ago, in the second year after the Wall fell. Our route took us along freshly asphalted streets that no longer made drivers fear for the axles of their cars, painted with gleaming white stripes down the middle (although tonight these were covered by the fog), while the trees of the avenue dropped past us to the left and right. The cones of our headlamps still showed the trees very clearly but right behind them we saw only vague, washed-out forms, like a row of sheets drifting in the wind. The woman sitting next to me leant forward, her hands grasping the steering wheel so tensely that her knuckles stood out, her hair was combed back and held at the nape with a hairclip but a strand had come loose and hung at the side. Although she had known this road well for years now, she kept turning her head here and there to get her bearings. Her otherwise mild and sleepy-seeming face looked unaccustomed, stern and wakeful and I couldn't help wondering whether she really was the woman I knew or whether, perhaps, the woman I had known had merely affected that mild and sleepy manner. But then I thought that it had to be something to do with the light, a half-light that made the otherwise imperceptible lines on her face seem carved in stone, a light in which every frown or wrinkle showed as a shadow. Or else, I had been so infected by the town's reticent, tight-lipped manner, their way of never quite saying all that they mean, that I no longer trusted anyone.

At last she found our junction, turned off the street onto a forestry road paved with concrete slabs, and from here we went downhill, as much as downhill meant anything hereabout where every slight elevation was called a hill, and I knew that we were headed for the Spree, having left the forest behind us by now. I could hear the woman humming faintly as she beat her hand against the wheel, then realized that it was not humming but moaning. She was moaning in a way that might be mistaken for humming. I wound my window down and there was the smell of burning, not unpleasant, rather like the smell of potato halms burning after the harvest. There was still nothing to see but the fog and in it, a few scattered willows, showing that we were near the water. The fog reached up to their lower branches so that they could have been mistaken for broad, spreading bushes standing on a hill. The Spree spread out at this point until it was almost a lake, its right bank curving out in a great sweep so thickly grown with reeds that there was no way to tell where the river ended and the land began. There were the meadows and then the reeds, and as you walked toward them birds took wing. You had dry ground under your feet until, with one more step, you were upto your knees in water and the reeds that you had just been looking across now blocked your view.

I knew from my grandfather that pike lurked in such waters, hanging among the stems of the reeds and waiting for their prey.

The road turned left and by now it was a simple sandy track, leading back along the forest's edge. We had left the concrete slabs behind, the forest was to our right, the reed-skirted water meadow to our left, the car bumped over ruts in the earth and over roots branching and twisting through the soil, and when I leant out of the window, there was the sharp smell of smouldering rubber. Now there were swirls of smoke mixed with the fog, creeping across the ground. Then a row of tall poplars, a fence and, on the other side of the poplars, several low fires, as though seen through frosted glass. The woman stopped but left the motor running, she toppled forward and hit her head against the steering wheel. 'Come on, then!' But she remained sitting where she was, without stirring, face down, eyes shut, as though refusing to get out or even to look. Her arms hung down, her head lay on the wheel, I leant forward and saw her eyeballs turn upward under the lids.

The dashboard clock showed half past twelve, eighteen minutes had passed since the knock on my door, I had looked at my watch. Who's that, at such an hour? And when I opened the door, the woman was standing there in the stair-well, alone, without her husband, which was remarkable right away, since I never saw one of them without the other. She had not been able to find the light switch, had fumbled her way up the stairs in the dark and yelled at me straight-away that I should come with her, right away, but I was in my dressing gown, had just been sitting down to write my final report, had already undressed, so she had to wait a moment. 'What's going on?' She followed me along the hallway into the room with the pictures and the desk spread with charts and tables. 'What is it?' I asked again, at which she looked at me calmly (striking in itself, after the yelling at the door) and said, 'Konrad.'

'What about him?'

But she had already turned away and had begun scurrying about. I switched off my desk lamp and went into the other room. While I dressed the door was ajar, so that I could see her running round among the pictures leaning up against the walls in that room. She usually wore cream clothes, loosely draped, but this evening she was wearing a pair of dark trousers, a green windcheater and jogging shoes which squeaked with every step and as she paced and squeaked she muttered the words nervous breakdown, fit of rage, Konrad, and flung her arms out wide to bring them back together again and smack the heels of her hands together, while I took my parka from where I had packed it, from the suitcase where it lay atop folded trousers, shirts and pullovers.

What was I doing, back then? Observing the water levels and conditions for navigation? Was I an agent for a shipping line that wanted to sound out the upper Spree for business, their business, back then in the days when everything was in flux? Cap'n, is it worth investing in a particular type of shallow-draught boats, given that they would not be profitable carrying under one hundred passengers, and is it worth constructing a chain of quays up that stretch of the river to Berlin? Yes, that's what I was doing. I had been lodged in two rooms in a castle used as a museum and I shared the larger room with a number of paintings which in earlier times had hung in the government offices, factories, schools and cultural

centres of a now vanished state and which the museum director had now collected to protect from loss or damage, bringing them to this castle.

A new van-load of pictures arrived every week and the
janitor carried them up the steps and leant them against the
walls. One of them was called 'The Boat Trip' and showed a
converted lighter with its loading hatch covered and benches
set out where the hatch had been. Black-clad men and women
sat on the benches, looking dead ahead in the direction of
travel. The boat was shown from side-on and the passengers
sat so neatly in line that it was as though an invisible cord
were stretched along the row of figures. I have forgotten the
artist's name but I remember that the museum director, a tall,
lean man with a deeply lined brow and hair standing out
wildly all over his head, told me that the artist had fallen out
of favour after producing this picture, had been forbidden to
show in exhibitions, received no more commissions, espe-
cially since these people turned up in all his paintings after
that. I learnt that he had been well known in the Sixties for
light-hearted scenes—'First Day of School', 'The Holiday
Camp'—but then, in the early seventies, the black-clad figures
had become his main theme, or, rather, he had continued to
paint bright, cheerful scenes but these were now overshad-
owed, as though against his will, by the black figures in the
background or at the edges of a picture, so that the scene's
good cheer was turned on its head.

And she was standing in front of this picture, 'The Boat
Trip', when I came back. She leant forward and narrowed her
eyes, then, when she heard me approach, straightened up
sharply and turned to face me and there was a hunted look
in place of her usual mild and sleepy expression. 'Where are

we going?' Instead of answering, she looked at the painting one last time and hurried out through the door, not speaking until we were in the car, where she said that he was in the cabin (or did she say dacha?).

To the garden then, where they had always wanted to take me ever since I had arrived. Since I arrived? No, since we had been running together. They had been running for years, they were both teachers and Konrad was also a sportsman, an athlete, a runner, while I had only begun here in town, from boredom. 'Tommy, you'll like the garden.' Be that as it may, every time they invited me I came up with some excuse—an existing commitment, my work, the trips I took to make charts and take soundings, tedious calculations involving depths and currents. It wasn't that though. The garden was outside town, could only be reached by car and I didn't have a car. I felt just as my grandfather did, who only ever agreed to visit places that he could leave by his own means and whenever that couldn't be done he always felt trapped. Or was it instead because of Konrad, the way he fixed me with his dark eyes as we talked, eyes that thirsted for justice, as though he expected me to speak some redeeming word that would explain to him why history had run this course and no other? How could I explain the world when all I knew was ships, river flow rate and payload?

The bridge was clear but fog hung over the river. On both sides of the bridge, exactly in the middle, lanterns burnt, or, rather, one had been smashed days ago. Two men stood beneath it with their backs to the railings and as we drove past they bent to look into the car and when I turned in my seat, they were walking away. Right after that the road curved, a sign declared *Eisenhüttenstadt 25 km*, and now we were out of town and driving along the edge of the meadows that separated us from the river and we passed into the pine forest. She stared ahead, her hands clenched on the steering wheel and whenever I asked her why Konrad had had this nervous breakdown or fit of rage, she shook her head or gave such a tight-lipped answer that I gave up asking and stared out instead at the fog, creeping and drifting on the road and between the trees. She tucked strands of hair away from her eyes, strands which fell back straightaway, and now the hunted look on her usually mild, sleepy face gave way to that watchful, hard expression I had never seen before and I wondered why she had asked me to go with her—the truth was that we were mere chance acquaintances—but by then she had turned off the highway into the back road.

Now the smell of petrol joined the smells of fog and smoke. I yanked the door open and at that same moment, a flame shot up, there was a deafening blast, followed by several more, smaller explosions, something swept over me, then total silence, as though I had been plunged into water. The woman had got out and was running after me. A torch beam danced through the fog and hanging smoke, in the next moment I saw the torch fall, shining on the grass now. The woman had fallen, she got up (leaving the torch where it was) but hardly was she on her feet than she collapsed again. She yelled, 'My ankle!' and now we could hear the wood crackling, and the air was full of flying sparks. Crackling of flames and sparks thick and fast and all at once the realization that he could be lying somewhere in there, the gaunt man with the aquiline face and the body pared down by running countless miles, the man who could put on such a burst of speed, when he chose, that he left me standing like a rooted tree. In the seventies he had won the 800-metre student championships in East Germany, setting a time that should have entitled him to take part in the national championships, but the invitation never came, he watched the championships on television instead and saw the winner come in with a time well above his own personal best. If he had been allowed to take part he would have won or been among the front-runners which in turn would have qualified him for that year's Olympics, foreign travel, international fame—all that, if only it hadn't been denied him for reasons that he still brooded over with the tenacity peculiar to those who had been robbed of their life's goal, speculating as to his offence (his big mouth, his 'socially corrosive attitudes').

'Tommy!' The woman had hobbled up to join me, hanging on to my arm, the firelight reflected on her face from the flames that blazed some fifteen yards away, sending out an intolerable heat until the cabin or dacha collapsed and the big fire fell in on itself and dwindled. The smaller fires that we had seen from the car were only glimmering points of light scattered across the whole garden, lost in its depths—all these fires were tidy little heaps of tinder, carefully prepared, now burnt down. He had cut down all the bushes and poured petrol over them, thrown furniture and fittings from the cabin into their branches, the chairs, the table, the mattresses, the contents of the cupboards. I walked past these and carefully rummaged round with my foot in the seared and charred remains while the woman stared into the darkness, standing still. She looked toward the forest as though she expected him to come out from between the trees any moment. She was probably right, or so I think today, since although I searched the garden and grounds several times I couldn't find him anywhere. Either he had run to the road or he was still standing somewhere at the edge of the darkness, watching while we stumbled round the garden. I took a rake that was lying about and broke up the smouldering wood, went down to the river and washed soot from my hands— my hands and arms were black to the elbows and one sleeve on the parka was torn where I had pulled it up. The fog hung over the water, further away I could hear a plopping sound as though a fish had sprung out of the water and dived back.

A few days before, I had found a place on the other side of the river that fitted exactly into the plans of the shipping company who employed me, not on one of my surveying trips along the Spree but on one of my evening runs. Konrad had gone to Berlin for an appointment with the authorities, Stasi headquarters in Normannenstrasse and since his wife never went running without him I didn't take their usual route through the forest but jogged along the riverbank and found a spot where the land jutted out into the water a little, not marsh or reed bank that would require draining but dry ground that would only need a little levelling and shoring up. As soon as the land fell away, the water reached a depth of two and a half metres, so that there was hardly any need to bring in the dredgers, an advantage that I mentioned in the final report I drew up that same evening.

After I dropped the woman off at the castle, I never saw her again. I called the museum director to ask about the picture, which I wanted to buy, but he turned me down, explaining that the collection could not be broken up. He also told me that she had quit teaching, sold her furniture and moved back in with her mother somewhere in Thuringia and as he said this I thought that I could hear something like satisfaction or scorn in his voice.

Weeks later, back in Berlin, I was walking across the Jannowitz Bridge one evening when I noticed a man in a black leather jacket leaning over the railings. He was propped up on outstretched arms and gazing at the water and when I followed his gaze I saw a decommissioned boat tied up to the wall below, probably on its way to the breaker's yard. The seating had been ripped off from the deck and one of the doors to the bridge was hanging loose on its hinges, held closed by a chain through the doorhandles. And all at once I noticed that I was being watched, that the man in the leather jacket was looking at me, had turned to face me. It was Konrad. He lifted his hand, palm outward, as though to show me that if I spoke a word he would shove it back down my throat, then he slapped the railings, turned round and crossed to the S-Bahn station.

And all of a sudden I remembered their first visit to the castle. We were sitting in the picture gallery, with the window open in front of the desk, we could see the rain. Konrad said, 'We've brought you something,' and she fished round in her willow basket, took out a jar of honey and put it on the table among all the maps, charts and calculations. 'Home-made,' she said, and he, 'Not by us,' she, 'By a bee-keeper,' he, 'A neighbour,' she, 'Whose bees come into our garden.' That was their way of speaking, not interrupting but mutually completing, embellishing or ending one another's sentences, a habit that had grown into a sort of antiphony or duet, as though two people were thinking one thought or one person speaking from two mouths.

When they left, I went to the window. The courtyard was strewn with holes where the water had pooled. They had linked arms and were jumping over the puddles and his right hand held the umbrella to shelter her from the rain that suddenly came down more strongly. They jumped together, landed together and because they kept their arms linked the whole time, it looked odd, like some kind of very difficult move in figure skating, almost impossible to master.

five

GLENDENNING

Tonight, when I reach the end where the asphalt track peters out into tussocky grass, light sweeps past, a washed-out glare of headlamps, the sky above the strip of forest behind this field glows for a moment and straight after that I hear a muffled roaring and know that the light is from a truck ploughing along on the highway behind the hill with the windmills, through the rain and the dark. The driver has pulled the chain that sounds his horn. As a warning? For fun? To tell his lover who lives nearby that he is driving past? Here I am. Can you hear me?—Perhaps she is embracing the cushion and her thoughts fly out to him—if only he would stop!—while I, standing in the middle of a sodden field in Lower Saxony, hear the roar and find myself hurled onto the street at Hoboken, strewn with tiny shards of toughened glass, on the pier across from the southern tip of Manhattan, the street where the truckers parked their cabs.

Yes, now I see the *Mildred*, the ship I worked on at the time. Once the containers were loaded the truckers would stick the dockets into the breast pocket of their overalls and climb into their cabs and as they turned into Water Street, away from the pier, the horn would howl, goodbye then, and Dave, master on the *Mildred*, wouldn't leave this unanswered, a matter of honour, he'd pull the siren chain so that every time a truck turned into Water Street its roar flew through the streets of Hoboken, echoing far out across the Hudson.

And now the layout of the truck stop where we lodged comes into focus, the lodgings we boatmen shared with the truckers (those of us who didn't sleep onboard), and I can see the little man who came toward me at the forecourt entrance one day, a dull, rainy day like today, walking with spry, bouncing steps. He headed toward me, stopped right in front of me, looked at me and said his name, 'Glendenning, Bill Glendenning.' And when I introduced myself in turn— 'Thomas,'—he shook his head. He had a thin face, lined and furrowed with wrinkles, and light, watery eyes. He looked up at me, his face came closer to mine, he stood on tiptoes and repeated, putting a pause after each syllable, 'Glendenning.' And when I nodded he turned away and skipped off to the shacks at the other end of the forecourt. At the door he turned round and looked at me and, then and there, I knew that I hadn't passed the test. Whatever challenge he had set me, I had failed. I understood that from the way he looked at me. At the same time I felt something like sadness, disappointment, not unlike what I saw in my grandfather when I could not answer his questions. He would say, 'How are things at the Dogleg, the Calm Before, the Cant Hook?' Pubs or, as he called them, hostelries which had once been sited near locks or well-frequented mooring places but had been closed for a long time, had become dilapidated—at best you might still see their faded signs. When he mentioned these pubs (or hostelries) that too was some kind of test and when I failed it he would wave a hand dismissively and look at me, like the little man in Hoboken, with sadness and disdain in his eyes.

That evening I sat with the truck stop manager in the cafeteria, which was part of the place. He was so fat that he needed one of the little steel chairs for each of his buttocks and even then great wedges of meat hung over the edge of the seats left and right, only held in by his trousers. 'Glendenning,' I said, 'one of your staff is called Glendenning.' He thought about it for a moment, then told me I was wrong. 'We got fourteen people working in this stop, two mechanics, pump jockey, the two ladies run this cafeteria, two guards, all the rest are cleaners.' He leant against the back of the chairs, which squealed as they gave way, and shut his eyes as though calling to mind the face of every worker. 'Glendenning?' I described the man to him. But he didn't budge. 'No, you gotta be mistaken.'

Next morning we went up the Hudson to Poughkeepsie with a load of agricultural machinery and were supposed to take on gravel but since it took some time for us to unload our sister ship, the *Linda*, took the gravel while we came back with empty wooden crates, most of which broke as we were loading—splintered planks lay everywhere on deck, on the bridge and in the ways.

Once we were tied up again in Hoboken at about three in the morning, I went back to my room, but as I went down the passage in the dark (the lights were broken) I stumbled over a spar of wood wedged between the stanchions on the stairs and tumbled down the whole set. I lay there in shock for a while, then, when I sat up I felt a stabbing pain in my left hand and rolled onto my side. Dave came down the steps and when he pointed his torch at my hand we could see that the wrist was already swollen almost to the thickness of my upper arm. He took me to a clinic in Chambers Lane, where they X-rayed my arm and diagnosed a fracture above the wrist, too swollen to plaster up. The arm was strapped to a splint and bound up with damp cloths that smelt of herbs. By the time we left the clinic they had already dried to a hard crust.

'What next?' asked Dave. 'Where should I take you?'

Early November, half past six in the morning, the sun had just risen, twilight, a cold wind from the river. Since I had nowhere to live and would only be in everyone's way on the ship, I told him to drop me off at the truck stop. Dave thought for a moment, then stopped walking and said that I could have his flat (since he lived onboard anyway), which is how I came to Rivington Street.

Once we had fetched my suitcase from the ship, he drove me through the Holland Tunnel to Manhattan, a little along Broadway, then turned right onto Third Street. All of this (in my memory) runs together into a stream of events, when I was unconscious or nearly so, one thing leading to another, and this whole chain—the packing crates, the spar of wood on the stairway, the broken arm, Dave's offer of help—led to the moment when I saw the man from the truck stop again.

That evening I lay on my back in bed, looking at the ceiling, feeling the thrum and shake and shiver of the city that set me all a-jitter as well, as though I were in the belly of an ocean liner, but while the noises and movements on ship calmed me, the thrum and shake and shiver of the city set me on edge. I was in the city's rhythm or, rather, the city had a rhythm, its own beat, but my senses and my body were always a beat behind. You need to rest your arm, the doctor had said. Fine. But how, when the boom and screech and racket outside the window were echoing within me as though in an empty hold? I couldn't sleep and once I had got up again, it was past midnight, I thought I might just as well go out. I got dressed and put my arm in the sling, a piece of black cloth folded into a triangle and knotted at the ends, and since the lift was out of order (it was always out of order) I went down the stairs, where the flights were the colour of potato blight and a bare light bulb at the ceiling on every landing gave off a dim glow. It was so narrow on the stairs that two people could not pass. If anyone had come up the other way, then one of us would have had to squeeze up against the wall; no one came, I had the stairs to myself but when I turned off into one of the floors by mistake (where the hallways were wider, almost like little streets) I heard noises—talking, whispering, shuffling footsteps, scratching and scraping, a woman's voice singing softly, heaving, breathing or coughing, a regular tap-tap that moved about as though someone were testing the walls for cavities—as though from far off, yet quite distinctly.

I had left the Naval College six months before with my licence and had been sent here by the shipping company (which had some obscure connection with Hudson, Inc.) to learn about the switch-over from dry bulk to containers, an important task which, I was assured, the sister company in Newark knew all about and I could expect to be given a taste of all important aspects of the business. Then I was assigned to one of the oldest boats I had ever seen and instead of holding any position on board where my licence would have been of some use, against all my protests, I worked the ship as a kind of fourth man, lending a hand whenever there was a job to be done.

On arriving, I had reported to the company and had
boarded my assigned ship that same day. We had gone upriver to Poughkeepsie, Rhinebek, Albany, Troy, once up
through Newark Bay to the Hackensack River, so that I had
only ever seen Manhattan from across the river or from on
the river itself. Now I was on the island and tried to remember Dave's words. When we had turned off Broadway that
morning, we had crossed several wide streets, then finally
found ourselves among the smaller streets, or, let's say, ones
which were not quite so wide, where the houses were shabby
or derelict, or were only there as burnt-out shells or demoli-
tion sites. I looked out of the window while I listened to his
voice, soft, almost without inflection. I was in my early twen-
ties, he was ten years older, and I remember that he gave me
advice like an older brother, all sorts of warnings about the
city, the neighbourhood, the house, the flat itself—if someone
knocks on the door, put the chain on before you open, shut
the window before you go out because of the fire escape (they
climb in that way), don't give yourself away on the street as
from out of town, meaning, don't dress too well, don't walk
too slowly, don't stop for no reason, don't gawk about or
gape at things like a hick. Just walk without looking up, hus-
tle, look like you know where you're going. Is it still like that
today? That's how it was back then at least, in the early seventies, and I thought of all this, of Dave's words, as I undid
the two locks and opened the front door.

Yellow light lay in the streets, a red–black sky glowed
above the rooftops. Blank-eyed boys leant in entranceways,
their hands cupped round cigarettes. A shop was still open
(grocery? drugstore?), with the door ajar but a grille let down
in front of it, from behind which I saw an old woman look

across at me with sleepy eyes. At the corner of Rivington & Ludlow the neon light of a bar flickered green, I crossed the street and as I went in I noticed a man who sat, back to the door, right at the end of the long bar that ran the length of the room. The place was almost empty. Just that man, an older couple sitting at a low glass table (etched with an advertisement for Chivas Regal) and the barkeep, a young girl who looked up from a thick book lying open behind the counter and hurried to the beer tap when I gave my order, while the man looked over his shoulder. He looked across at me from the other end of the bar and although it was dark (candlelight only) I recognized him, the man from the truck stop—now I recalled his name, Glendenning, no doubt about it. I waved to him, while he stared at my sling. I waved again but he looked aside. On the way to the toilet, I passed him. 'Mr Glendenning?' At which he turned round, briefly, then turned away again immediately. 'We met at the truck stop.' He lifted his glass, drank, put it down and said that he didn't remember. 'In Hoboken.' He said he'd never been there. 'But you're Mr Glendenning.' No, he told me, he wasn't, there must be some mistake.

This evening he was wearing a suit, white shirt, open collar, a grey coat lay on the stool next to him. As I came back from the toilet I saw him take the coat and go to the door, at which I paid and followed him. He turned into Ludlow, it was round half past one in the morning, the street was empty, the shops shut, the iron blinds let down. He walked close to the buildings, hands in his pockets. Some mistake? No, not a chance. The wrinkled face, the clear eyes, the brown hair streaked with white and, of course, the way he walked, that

odd, sprightly, hopping gait, which sent him shooting up into
the air with every step, landing again straightaway.

I followed him at a distance of about fifty metres. Sometimes the shadows of the houses swallowed him so completely that I thought I had lost him, then they spat him out
again at the next streetlamp or lit window. The next window?
In fact, there was only one window still lit, a shop window,
the shop itself seemed to be open, the light fell on the pavement and I saw him in this light. He came out of the shadow
of the houses into the light, looked in through the window,
went on, back into the shadow once more, and was lost for
good now. I went as far as the next corner and then turned
back to the shop where I had lost him. A shop? There were
words on the window in two lines, two curving arcs of writing that didn't quite meet, the one above saying *Reader*, the
one below, *Advisor*, and between the two the outline of a
hand in green neon. A fortune-teller. Glendenning had
stopped in front of a palmist's shop window, a soothsayer.
The walls of the room were draped with bolts of black cloth
that fell in sharp, even folds. In the middle of the room stood
a table with two chairs, the red velvet tablecloth fell right to
the floor and at the middle of the table a crystal ball which
shone with a white light, and (apart from the neon-tube
hand) this was all that lit the room, which was empty, just
the table, the two chairs, the globe and a white sheepdog
lying in front of the black draperies at the back, his head on
his paws. Suddenly, he raised his head and when he looked
at me I involuntarily took a step backwards not because he
frightened me but because I felt myself observed, recognized
as a snooper. I can't describe it except by saying that there
was something indifferent and at the same time mocking,

knowing, in the way he looked at me, as though he had expected me—although no one in the city even knew me, although I had never been in this street before—expected me in front of this window at exactly this hour of the night.

Next to the window, set back a little and already in the shadow, there was a door with the same emblem, the two curving lines of script and the neon hand. Had Glendenning gone in to the fortune-teller's? I tried the handle but the door was locked. It was a glass door with a dark curtain behind it, no way to see through, and the black dot of a bell push on the wall beside it. I lifted my hand, dropped it again and walked on, only to turn back straightaway. There was a yellow sheet of notepaper taped above the bell push, bearing not a name but a short text, four or five lines of archaic-seeming English, which I had seen by the flame of my cigarette lighter. The words? I had forgotten them already but suddenly thought that I should memorize them. I stepped up to the door again, flicked the lighter once more and read, until it got so hot that I burnt my hand. *It is an easy thing to talk of patience to the afflicted, to speak the laws of prudence to the houseless wanderer. While our olive and vine sing and laugh round our door. And our children bring fruits and flowers.* What was that? A message? For whom? On the way back home, I muttered the words to myself until I had them by heart and once I was back in Rivington I wrote them on a sheet of paper and hung it on a nail above the kitchen table. By now I had been on my feet for almost forty hours, I lay down on the bed fully dressed and fell asleep straightaway, only waking up at noon with noise filling my skull.

The sun was glaring through the window, the blare and screech and racket came up from the street and below that I could hear a sort of counterpoint, the sound of footsteps flapping and slapping as though a sandalled horde were being chased through the building, but when I opened the door carefully, just a crack, I saw the girls who ran along the hallway past my door, turning about, running back, then the other way, back past my door, pell-mell, four or five young girls, all of them in tight miniskirts and thin, see-through T-shirts or shirts, their small breasts showing through, and on their feet, not sandals but pumps, which made that flapping, slapping sound on the stone floor, echoing off the walls.

Across from my door, through the crack I could see two boys leaning against the wall, the same age as the girls (between fifteen and twenty), each with a leather whip in his hand, which they cracked every now and again by raising an arm and snapping it down—no, rather it was a motion of the wrist, a lazy flick of the hand that was enough to set the whip snapping through the air and send the girls rushing off again. They lashed the air and the snap chased after the girls and now I saw that the girls were ramming elbows into one another's ribs, barging and shoving at one another or kicking at legs and ankles until the first, the girl who had managed to get a little ahead of the others, stumbled and fell, the others jumping over her and past. Two of them were white, the other two or three I thought were Puerto Rican, like the boys.

The girl who had fallen stayed where she was and when the others came back fleeing, she grabbed at their legs and hit out so that one of them, trying to dodge, lurched, twisted an ankle, fell down, and as she fell brought down with her the girl running alongside, while the last of them (there were only four after all) stopped, panting, then fought her way through the hands that snatched and slapped at her from the floor. She kicked at them, short, neat kicks that brought her through the mob, and when she reached a clear piece of floor a whistle shrilled out down the hall to announce that the race was over.

One of the boys, the taller, had whistled sharply between his teeth. The other reached into his shirt, drew out a bundle of banknotes, riffled through it, took out a couple of notes and gave them to the taller boy, who stuck them in his belt. The short boy went to the girl who had fallen first and held out the stock of his whip toward her. She grabbed it, pulled herself up but then fell down again and stayed sitting where she was. The other two had got up, they were leaning against the wall with their hands to their sides. The winner came back, kicked the red pumps off her feet and squatted, at which the tall boy who had won the money stepped behind her and stroked her neck. She gulped in some air, lifted her head and nestled her cheek into his hand, turned to put her face into his hand, he drew his hand away and she moved her head after it. When her head touched his hand the boy pushed her away and grabbed her hair. He hauled her up and when she was on her feet he put his hand round her waist, his arm was right round her, hand on her belly, and in his other hand hung the whip, and joined like this they passed out of sight and the losers of the race followed them.

Was there a word spoken, even a single word? No, just the crack of the whip, the flapping and slapping, gasping, coughing. I don't know whether what came next was something I actually saw or whether it was part of a dream that I had later. Hardly had they left my view than the girl who had fallen first came back, a stick-thin brown girl with a garish green shirt that ended above her navel. She came into sight and bent down for the red pumps that the winner had left there. She picked them up, held them tenderly to her bosom and gyrated her hips, danced forward two steps, back two, two to each side, she rocked the shoes at her bosom the way a mother rocks the child she has just lifted from bed and then, utterly unexpected—a polecat devouring a chick—she sank her teeth into them. Her small sharp face turned toward me, my eye at the crack of the door, not even two metres from her, but I do not think that she saw me. Her head flung from side to side while her hands tore at the shoes until they hung in tatters from her lips.

A dream? If so, then one so closely bound up in my memory with everything else I saw that it has become part of the scene on Rivington Street. Even now, years later, on the asphalt path at night, in the middle of rain-sodden fields in Lower Saxony, in rain that falls more heavily now, I can see the girl in the hallway, the red tatters in her hands, between her teeth. A dream? I know for sure that I saw her again in the hall where the people sat humming—she stood at Glendenning's left hand, he himself sat a little higher up, on a sort of throne, while the dog that had led me to them curled up at his feet like a snail.

Dave's flat had two rooms, one with a bed in the front, looking over the street, then the other at the back. It was both his study and his kitchen and its window looked out onto the lightwell. The shelves on his wall were made of stacked breeze blocks with planks between and held two books that had been on the curriculum at the Naval College. *The Navigation of Flat-Bottomed Boats* and *The Deep*. After I had leafed through these for a while, I sat down and wrote a letter to the shipping company, which I should have written some time ago, but had been putting off because I enjoyed the sailing (Oh Hudson, the dark slopes of your shores). I wrote that I saw no prospect of attaining the skills they expected me to acquire as long as I was employed as a spare pair of hands on a boat which would have been retired from service long ago back home and I ended by saying that in the circumstances, I would have to ask to be recalled. I did not mention my accident since it seemed to me that this would only emphasize my failure—for failure it was. Then I made coffee, went into the front room, lay down on the bed and fell asleep straightaway, only waking in the evening when the telephone rang. It was Dave. He asked how I was. Fine, I said. He was calling from Poughkeepsie, where they had stopped on the way up to Albany with engine trouble.

Meanwhile it had got dark. The neon light from the street rose up high, rain was streaming past the window and when I went into the kitchen, my eyes fell on the words which I had read by the fortune-teller's bell push and which I had written down on a sheet, *It is an easy thing to talk of patience to the afflicted*, and I thought that they (and the rest) needed something to complete them. But what? What might come after?

The refrigerator was empty, so I went downstairs. There were a number of shops on Rivington, delis kept by Latinos or Koreans, their wares set out under the awnings on the pavement. But instead of buying anything I kept walking, then turned into Ludlow a little way on. Now, in the early evening—it must have been around seven o'clock—the neon sign was switched off and the curtain was drawn, I almost walked past but then I saw the outline of the hand, bracketed by the two lines of text and stepped up to the door and flicked my lighter. The yellow notepaper was gone, in its place hung a sheet of red paper which also had a few lines on it. *Then is forgotten the slave grinding at the mill, and the captive in chains, and the soldier laid groaning among the happier dead. It is an easy thing to rejoice in the tents of prosperity. To see a God on every wind.*

'Mr Glendenning?'

I turned with a start and saw a black man, buried under a heap of blankets and towels, sitting in a little cart with cardboard stuffed into the sides as insulation. His naked feet stuck out at the front. He was wearing a brown peaked cap with yellow trim, like the porters in the big hotels wear, and had cords and chains round his neck, with various objects attached—a bicycle bell, a pocket watch, mussels, feathers, several sizes of key. There was a long pole lying slantwise across the blankets and towels and an umbrella stuck between the spokes, which he had not opened even though the rain was heavier now.

'Mr Glendenning,' he repeated in a high, sing-song voice. 'Mr Glendenning, sir, pardon me for not recognizing you right away.' He took his cap off as he said this and bowed, as far as he could from a sitting position. He lowered his head, while he put the hand holding the cap onto the chaos of blankets and towels.

'We were expecting you already.' There was the same light in his eyes as I had seen in Glendenning's. 'But we didn't know where you'd be, that's to say, how you'd be joining us. That's why I was waiting at the bus station, little ol' me, and Ed, Edward Safran, he was keeping an eye out for you at Grand Central. Mr Hobbes was convinced you'd be coming over the river, he's been watching the docks and the truck stops for weeks now. But now . . .' He was babbling, the words tumbling out of him as though after prolonged fear or an exertion which had given way now to relief. 'If you would be so kind . . .' He picked up the long pole that lay over his mess of blankets and towels and pushed himself down the street, using it as though he were in a canoe, steering with his feet that grasped the upright shaft of his little cart.

I walked behind him and for a while the only sounds were the drumming of the rain and the squeaking wheels of the cart. At the end of the block he turned into a driveway, a tunnel through a building that led to a large courtyard and then through another such arch into a smaller yard. We crossed several yards, with him leading the way in his cart-canoe, and every time we entered a new courtyard and he turned round I thought that I should correct his mistake. When we had got to the fifth or sixth yard, I saw a white shape, the dog that had looked at me from the fortune-teller's studio—it seemed to be waiting for us. It sat there, ears pricked up, listening, looked at us as we arrived and as we reached it, got up and walked ahead of us. It was—have I said this already?—completely dark, no light coming from any of the buildings round the yard and the rain drowning the noises of the city with its din. The sky was rust-red where it showed above the rooftops. The white dog, the man punting himself along (who had fallen silent once we entered these courts), then myself, all just a few metres apart, and when we entered the eight or ninth courtyard, I saw light at the ground-floor windows. The curtains were drawn but did not quite cover the windows, so that sharp wedges of light pierced the darkness from the gaps at the sides.

The dog slipped through the door and when the man with the pole turned round, a wedge of light fell across his face and I saw a look that even today I can only call reverential or awestruck. His mouth was shut but a humming arose from his ribcage like the sound of a large insect sitting somewhere inside him. Indeed, since the dog had slipped through the door, the same humming reached us here outside, many voices, strong and loud, rising and falling in waves (a swarm of hornets?). The man, little ol' him, bowed once more and showed me the door with his hand, to indicate that if I pleased I should go in ahead of him.

Was it an abandoned gym we walked into? In any case, I remember climbing bars on the walls, a horizontal bar, rings hanging from the ceiling, barres and springboards pushed together into a corner and crash mats piled up. The rows of chairs were completely full, right up to the last seat, with an aisle left free in the middle. When I came in, the people stood up and put their hands together, turning their faces to me and there I saw the same reverence or awe as on the canoe man's face.

The dog sat behind the door and looked at me with its amber eyes, its head slightly cocked to one side as though waiting for a sign. The humming had swelled to become a polyphony, a chorale, and I thought that I caught fragments of hymns. Had I stumbled into the meeting of a religious sect?

There was a low podium at the short end of the hall, opposite the door, with a few steps leading up to it and there I saw Glendenning or, rather, the man I had thought was him, though in fact he had to be the one that the canoe man had called Hobbes, the one who had been waiting for a man called Glendenning in Hoboken. Glendenning, Bill Glendenning, he hadn't been introducing himself when he said that but asking a question. He was draped in a robe made of scraps and patches sewn together and sat on an armchair that had been decked out with all kinds of gewgaws to look like a throne—bicycle inner tubes, gold-coloured, had been wound about the curved legs, there seemed to be flowers growing from the backrest, plastic flowers, I realized, stuck to the wood, and the armrests ended in clocks, large old-fashioned alarm clocks, their faces to the congregation.

Hobbes was the only one who stayed seated while the two girls who sat a little lower down the three-tiered podium had also got up. I recognized one of them as the sharp-faced girl, her shocking-green blouse shirt out at me. The other girl was white and so fat that her upper thighs rubbed together even though she had straddled her legs apart, her small chin was sunk deep into the rolls of fat on her neck and I found myself thinking of the truck-stop manager I had talked to about Glendenning. She held a velvet cushion in her hands with a watch, the same I had seen on the canoe man, the same size and design, although this one was worth much more. His watch had been of brushed steel while this one was gold, with little glittering stones, red and green, set in the casing. And now I realized that the others were wearing watches as well, on cords or chains round their necks, and as I went past them, they lifted the watches and held them out toward me like some sort of token. Although these were nothing but plain over-the-counter watches, run-of-the-mill shoddy things, nevertheless they seemed to be the only things of any value that these people owned. Their clothes were what my grandfather would have called well-looked-after, meaning that they had no rips or patches but also that there was something scrimping, sad, drab about them. Neat and tidy are poverty's brother and sister, they make poverty more obvious and also give it a meaning, saying that you should never draw attention to yourself, never be extravagant. Even if here and there I saw little patches of colour, nevertheless the overall impression was grey—jackets, trousers, pullovers, coats, shoes, bags, all in the various shades of grey. And a grey, driven look etched onto their features, a tiredness, relieved only by the ecstasy of my arrival (or rather, Glendenning's) that lit up their faces. Reverence, wonder, awe, rapture—I have spent a long time looking for the word that would describe the expression on their faces. I think that it's rapture, nothing else will do. They turned faces filled with joy toward me, held the watches up to me and I think that it would not have taken much for the steady humming that rose from their ribcages to have lifted them from the floor and set them swaying in the air.

The dog walked in front of me and when we reached the podium it lay down and curled up. Hobbes stood up and came toward me in that patchwork quilt of a robe. He came down the steps at a stately pace, took my hand and led me up the steps, then when we were at the top he took off the robe and draped it about my shoulders. At his signal, I sat down where he had been enthroned. A second signal and the girl with the velvet cushion approached. Hobbes took the watch and lifted it high and the humming stopped abruptly and in the sudden silence he began to speak, his voice ringing out like thunder: 'Dearly beloved sisters and brothers'—and in his sermon, he had the most astonishing trick of switching from one language to another in mid-sentence, without the slightest break, English, Spanish, German, French, Dutch,

Russian (or Polish), a few more that I did not know. As far as I could understand what he said, the Promised One had arrived and thus the time of preparation had come to an end and the time itself now had come. I listened and at the same time I noticed how my thoughts wandered. I saw myself in Greenwich, walking the towpath, the next moment I stood at the canal and heard the clinking as my grandfather kicked the iron ring where his boat had been tied up, then hardly had that sound died away than the hoot of the truck horns roared in my ears and the *Mildred*'s siren joined in, so that at once I saw myself standing in the Hoboken streets and then the next moment floating high above the Hudson, Newark, Manhattan, and now, in the next picture, I was tripping over the slat and tumbling downstairs and saw myself going to the clinic with Dave. And as the last picture showed, I heard many voices speak, Amen, voices from the congregation raised in response to Hobbes.

'Amen.'

'Mr Glendenning?'

The girl in the lime-green blouse was kneeling in front of me and when I looked up, I saw Hobbes walk down the aisle, a little man in a grey suit whose only remarkable feature was that he hopped or skipped a little with every step. He skipped along the aisle, the others had stood up, and when he reached the last row of chairs the people left their rows and joined him, then those from the second and third rows, until there was a long line. They followed Hobbes out into the courtyard. Within a few minutes, the hall was empty. I was still wearing the robe, sitting on the chair and suddenly, I understood that though I was the Promised One, no one needed me.

'Mr Glendenning, sir?'

The girl gave me her hand and when she let go, I could feel something hard, cold—a small revolver, and in its chamber (as I found out later on Rivington) a single bullet. I still remember that once the girl had left as well, I somehow ended up on Ludlow where I bought a pound of bananas from a Korean.

The next morning I wrote the letter to the shipping company, then packed my bag, went down to the street and took a taxi to Hoboken. While we went through the tunnel I opened the newspaper that was lying on the back seat and read that there had been a number of coordinated attacks during the night. In Brooklyn, large parts of a refinery had gone up in flames, clearly arson, a car had been blown up near the stock exchange and the editor of a daily newspaer had been found shot dead in an underground car park. In all, there had been twenty-four fires, explosions and murders (the number of hours in a day), which had been attributed to one group, though there were no further details. I sat in the back of the taxi and as I read, I thought how easy it would be to change the rules of the game a little and instead of hours, use minutes or seconds or nanoseconds.

In Hoboken I took my old room in the truck stop and when I heard next morning that the *Mildred* had put in, I went on board and asked Dave to take me along as passenger. We loaded coke, bound for Albany. We cast off early in the evening. Since I couldn't be put to work, I sat in the forecastle, gripped by the fear that this could be my last voyage. At around eight o'clock we passed Peekskill, there was still a little light in the sky but by the time we went under the Bear Mountain Bridge, it was completely dark. Scattered lights showed on the steep forested slopes by the banks and I thought that this was the same river, the same mountains, that Hudson had seen from his ship, the *Half Moon*. A little later I spotted the lights of West Point and as we went by, I saw a name light up the eastern bank above us—Glendenning. The flames stretched over a hundred metres, each individual letter burning, each in flame, before the fire spread, first of all into the gaps between the letters and then to the forest all round. Dave came forward and said that the whole thing was probably an advertising stunt that had got out of hand. I knew better, although, of course, you could call it that as well.

I threw the revolver into the water just after Poughkeepsie and after we had put in at Albany, I left ship and took the first bus to Niagara Falls, where I crossed to Canada on foot. It was about seven in the morning when I got in the bus. The driver had turned on his radio and every few minutes they broadcast a description of Glendenning, though this only fit my appearance very slightly. I was worried though that the arm was mentioned—'last seen wearing a black sling over his left arm'—so that when I showed my passport, I said to the border guard, 'Perhaps I'm Glendenning.' He put a serious look on his face. 'Sir, that's nothing to joke about.' And he waved me on over the Rainbow Bridge into Canada.

Later I read that Hobbes was actually called Montferrat and had only adopted Hobbes as an alias so that he wouldn't stand out in the sect he had chosen. He was a New Zealander, of French descent, with a degree in chemistry. He had had a meteoric career in finance, worked as a lumberjack, then travelled to India. His destiny as a religious leader was foretold to him in a library where the holy texts were written on palm leaves. Just after Christmas, he was arrested on the same bridge that I had crossed that day in November. He was charged with conspiracy, arson and murder. The report in the *Toronto Star* didn't mention the name Glendenning, though the name must have been part of Montferrat's plans, even if it was only there to lay a false trail. Or was Glendenning a go-between, keeping in touch with other such groups? Was he expected because he was bringing a message? Or was the message in the simple fact of his arrival? Had Montferrat grown impatient when he didn't turn up and was that why he used me—perhaps there was some resemblance after all— to give the sign to begin? If that was the case, then he was the only one who could actually clear me of the suspicion of belonging to the sect, though I suspected I could not rely on him to be quite so generous. What if he decided to take me along on his last journey, which looked like being to the electric chair? It seemed to me wiser to keep what I knew to myself.

I saw the girl with the sharp face one more time, in Toronto, the evening when I heard that I should go back to Germany. I had been in the post office on Cecil Street where Dave forwarded my post and when I came out, she was waiting for me, still in that lime-green shirt, wearing several jackets over it but having fastened none of them. A baseball cap shadowed her dark face, pulled down low over her eyes, so that I only recognized her when she raised her head and said:

'Glendenning, traitor.'

Then she turned round and walked off fast toward Beverly Street and although my room was on Beverly, I felt it better to go in the other direction.

six

KATHARINA

Tonight, as I pull my boots on before going out into the fields, I catch sight of a picture in the hallway. Not a photograph, like the aerial view that shows me the houses arranged in a perfect circle but a print, as you sometimes find on the pages of a calendar, a reproduction of a painting, 'Café de la Marne', a multitude of swarming points of colour that conjure up an evening scene in a garden cafe. Clearly, rain has just fallen before, large scattered drops are falling from the trees onto the tables, so that some of the couples who sit there have put up their umbrellas. The benches, their clothes, the glasses, the cafe interior that lights up the garden, the guests with their faces turned expectantly toward the viewer, all of this in warm tones that still glow within me when, a little later, I step off the muddy asphalt path at the end of the village and hear— far off—dogs barking. In one of these villages huddling before the wind, sodden with the ceaseless rain, a dog starts barking, then another answers it from another village. A blurry light shows red on one of the windmills, their sails not turning and, all of a sudden, I see myself sitting on a bench in a similar garden cafe, the same expectant look in my eyes as the guests of Café de la Marne have, looking at us looking at the picture, though I am looking at the entrance to the garden.

It was many years ago. The cafe where I sat was not on a river, but on the avenue that leads, straight as an arrow, up to Charlottenburg palace in Berlin, where trees line the broad central strip. You can stand in the middle of the avenue and see the palace dome, where Fortuna balances on a golden globe.

A fine evening, warm, around ten o'clock, not quite dark yet, most benches taken, conversation humming like bees under a canopy of leaves. I had a table to myself but every few minutes people would come along and ask if they could sit there and every time I shook my head, 'No, there's someone coming,' which was true to the extent that I didn't want to rule out that she might come through the garden gate, the woman I was there to meet, the woman I was waiting for as I had waited for few women, the woman who did not come but let me wait, and it was not true to the extent that I had long ago stopped daring to hope to see her—which made it all the more important that I stay alone at my table, undisturbed, writing everything down.

Yes, I had got out a notepad and I remember now that it was marked with the crossed anchors of the shipping line I worked for at the time, and as my eyes darted back again and again to the garden gate, my thoughts drifted to the town on the canal, to the classroom in the big school building where our desks stood side by side, to my grandfather's house with the garden that ran down to the bank, to the brick-built villa where her parents lived—they had only moved into the town a little while before—to the room with the curious machines and up the stairs to her room where we had lain on the bed, that night, and then my thoughts leapt forward over all the years between.

On the afternoon of that day, the day I sat there, I had stopped to look at the posters on the window of a travel agency in Xantener Strasse—Faro, Djerba, Alicante, Cairo, Gizeh, the pyramids, and as my eyes drifted from the posters into the room beyond, I noticed a woman in her late thirties, my age, an employee, talking to a customer. Or did I not notice her until she had gone to the cupboard to fetch a stack of catalogues? Yes, I think it was this movement that broke the stillness in the room and drew my gaze inside from the posters, that was when I noticed her, the woman, the way she walked, something familiar in her walk. She was wearing a white blouse and dark-blue skirt, and when she turned round, I felt a pang pass through me.

It was Katharina, it was her, or, rather—better—she looked just like Katharina must look today. And when her customer came out, I went in. I entered the travel agency. She was tidying a sheaf of paper. She put it into a drawer, lifted her head and crossed her hands on the jotter.

'Can I help you?'

She had grey-green eyes, wreathed by tiny wrinkles, her hair, dark, was cut short, narrow hands, the little finger of the upper hand held a little in-turned. A name badge on the blouse with a name I did not know. 'Can I help you?' No, not her voice, her inflection. She looked at me with not a flicker of recognition, her gaze level, business-like, friendly. 'Yes?' And a minute later I was standing in the street again with a travel brochure I had asked for. If I had gone on then, which I didn't, the thing would have been over and done with. But I stayed where I was, looked through the window again and saw her leaning over a colleague's shoulder, an older woman with curly hair. She leant down and all of a sudden I recalled a remark my grandfather had made, *smoothly laggard*, by which he meant not just the way she walked, moved but also the way she talked, something drowsy in her speech, as though every word had to be wrung free from some deep-seated weariness, inexplicable in a girl so young—her voice, darkly nasal, drawled through every sentence until it suddenly (rarely) bubbled up into laughter and then returned to its level course. She walked smoothly, evenly, avoiding sudden stops or starts, as though some law dictated that every movement she made had to be followed through to the end, and the woman behind the window had this same gliding, even way about her. She straightened up, tucked her hair behind her ear at the same time (all in one motion with straightening up) and I knew that I would come back.

It was just after five o'clock. I went to Olivaer Platz, drank a cup of coffee at a snack bar and at six I was back in front of the travel agency, that's to say a little to one side, half hidden by an advertising column, and I saw it get dark behind the windows in that long, narrow room where the lights were always on even by day, saw the neon tubes switched off. A little after that her colleague left, the older woman with the curls, a light-brown shopping bag over her arm, and trotted off down Xantener. But Katharina (or the woman who looked just like her) did not appear and after a few minutes had passed, I went up to the window. She was sitting at her desk, back toward me, on the telephone, the receiver between her ear and her shoulder, holding down a sheet of paper with her left hand and writing something on it with her right. I could see the back of her head, her nape, her back and I thought of the mark that I had burnt into her shoulder, how she was branded on her left shoulder blade, just as I am branded on the right, three black dots in a triangle, that she had placed just so, so that (twist and turn as I might) I have never been able to see them or touch them with my hand but which I sometimes feel as an itch, a prickle, a steady pressure or a burning pain.

She put down the receiver, tore off the notepaper and put it in her pocket and as she stood up I went onward a little a step or two from the window, so that I could not be seen from inside the agency, but then stopped straightaway so that when she came out I could play the part of the chance passer-by (again). But when she came out, she turned the other way, so I had to walk behind her. I followed her as years ago I had followed Glendenning, or rather, Montferrat who had called himself Hobbes. The sun fell across the street. She walked fast, without losing any of the gliding smoothness (it almost looked as though she were rolling along on castors), in her white blouse and dark-blue skirt, with her bag over her shoulder, she looked less like a travel agent than a stewardess, back from across the seas, only the practical little suitcase missing to complete the image. She turned into Konstanzer Strasse, crossed the Kurfürstendamm at Olivaer Platz and stood at the bus stop. This was the moment when I could talk to her. But I hesitated and when the bus came, I climbed in after her. It was the 109 to the airport, my bus, the bus I took when I was in town and wanted to get back home. It went down the Kurfürstendamm, turned into Lewishamstrasse at Adenauerplatz, then went straight on across Kantstrasse and Bismarckstrasse, headed for the Charlottenburg bridge.

She sat two rows in front of me, gathered her hair back at the nape of her neck with a casual movement while I felt the itch on my back, on the spot that I can't reach. She had jabbed me a little off to the side, not on the shoulder as we had agreed but between the shoulder and the spine. Why? Why indeed? Did she enjoy inflicting pain? Was it a crazed wish to make her mark last forever or was it the opposite, the terror of time passing, the need to leave some mark, any? Was it to be sure that we would know one another if we were separated against her will, if we change beyond recognition? Perhaps. But nothing was said about any of this, for at the time, hardly a word was spoken, in my memory it is a time without words, a time when there were no words to comment on or explain what we did, wordless deeds that only meant anything, if they did at all, later. What we did, we did freely and any explanation came of its own accord. What happened, happened because it had to, not because of anything we had thought about or talked about beforehand—as that evening when she went to the cupboard, opened a drawer and took out (not without a certain trace of ceremony) a lighter, a needle and a bottle of ink, without a word, simply showing these three things, her gaze teasing and questioning, so that I had no choice, knowing that this would be the price, but to agree. No, that's wrong. At that moment I knew that this, just this, was what I wanted.

I nodded and we began to undress. She pulled her dress up over her head, turned round and showed me the place where I was to put the mark, turned again and began to unbutton my shirt, while she whispered, her mouth on my throat, that it had to be in the shape of a triangle, she needed that, hers point downward, mine point upward. It was dark in the room, she hadn't turned any lights on but the curtain was open, so that (standing where I was, my back to the door) I could see through the window, above her head, to the garden outside where it was a little lighter, trees outlined before a clear night sky. I put my right leg forward until it was between her legs, as though we were dancing, but she drew back, took the lighter and when she clicked the flame, the tree outside the window vanished. She let the candle wick catch the flame and put the candle on the floor beside the bed.

When we boarded, the bus had been full, the seats taken, people crowding the aisle, smelling of summer and sweat. It began to empty after Kantstrasse and the woman next to her got off. That was my chance to sit next to her. But it struck me that Katharina would have thought this an imposition. I saw her resting her head on the window, her head and shoulder touching the pane, then she sat up again and I remembered having to sweep aside her hair (she wore it long, back then). She lay stretched on the bed, her forehead on her hands, her hair spread out in a dark fan across her shoulders. When she stood up and wore her hair loose it reached down to her waist. I bunched it into my hand and swept it aside, it rustled gently.

The bus crossed Spandauer Damm, the palace to the left, the classical pavilion, then the river, the bridge, where I should get out, the bus stopped but I kept my seat. And now, looking ahead at the back of that neck, I remembered the hissing sound and the smell of burnt flesh. When I had heated the needle red-hot over the candle and plunged it into her skin, she arched and a tremor ran from her shoulders out across her back, shuddering waves over her back, her buttocks, legs, her feet which she had turned out to the side. Then she arched her body once more and the trembling lessened, subsided, died away. Her hands were stretched out at her sides and clenched and opened spasmodically. Of course, there was pain but the only sound she made was a sort of sigh, a deep exhalation, and she breathed out the words, 'The ink.' Now I had to rub the ink into the burn marks. I took the cap off the ink bottle, dipped my finger in, took it out and put it where she had instructed, *harder*, she groaned, harder, I should press harder, so that the black ink would seal into the burn, to be a lasting sign, a sign that would not wash away or vanish one day, fade as though it had never been. Or is this already making meaning from what we did? Yes, it seems to me, for in fact I cannot remember a word, only smells, images, sounds—the smell of her body at night, as I lay there with my face in the pillow I thought I caught a trace of that smell, a lingering hint, and when I turned my head aside, in the candlelight I saw that she had thrown our clothes over by the door. Thrown? No, she had rolled them up, bundled them together and put them against the bottom of the door to stop any sound from escaping (her parents slept two doors away).

One of these pictures is the staircase she led me down as day broke, her hand on the banister, her naked feet, the shirt over her shoulder where she bore the mark, early light on the treetops as we left the house, the leaves, already turning to their autumn colours, capped with light.

All this is part of it and the silence is part of the sounds I remember, the silence that gave way to thrashing and cracking as the dogs came out of the undergrowth, two deep-chested, powerful beasts which stopped at her command (a word? a signal?) and eyed us, obediently, yes, but truculent too, truculent in their obedience—it was clear that they would be upon me if her attention flagged for a moment.

Their short-haired pelts shone darkly, their flanks heaved, drool dripped from their jowls, lighter than the rest. Katharina bent down, closed her hands upon their leather collars studded with iron spikes, *Now go!*, and when I turned round in the driveway I saw her leaning back, her heels dug into the ground (a strap had slipped from her shoulder) as the dogs tore at their collars.

As I looked at the neck and shoulders of the woman who looked like Katharina, I realized that it was all inscribed in my memory, including the steep, dark path through the park-like garden, then the path that ran along the canal for a while and the smell of the canal too, a heavy, black smell, the grey heron (elegant, slender) sleeping on the jetty, the skirt of reeds, the water where the pike lurk, a gurgling sound as though bubbles were rising somewhere, and among all these images, sounds, smells, the joy of bearing that mark, rejoicing as though after passing an exam, now, as though now a new time began when we would never lose one another. Her triangle stood, its point down, mine point up.

I walked, and as I walked I realized that I was breathing, drawing air into my lungs, the blood was pounding in my ears and the burning on my back was on my skin too, all over my body. The grass was damp, my shoes showed dark patches, I put my hand in the grass and then under my shirt at the neck, trying to reach the burning, that spot that I know now, though I did not at the time, is unreachable, while the pictures filled my vision, the pictures of the house that until the previous evening I had only ever seen from outside. The red-brick villa with its numberless bays, balconies and turrets. A few steps led up to a front door, in the stonework above it a five-pointed star made of five unbroken lines, in the middle of this a G, for *gnosis* and *generatio*, knowledge and lineage. The villa had been built at the beginning of the century by the owners of the brickworks and had stood empty for years but now Katharina's family had bought it. One day, as winter ended, there was light behind the windows that had always been dark and a week later, the girl with the curious way of speaking had joined our class.

When Katharina had led me up the steps the evening before, we had come into a large hallway, where countless rooms led off and, I saw, led into one another as well by further doorways. She had taken my hand and gone through the first door, then another, a third and fourth. In every room we entered, the cupboards stood open and piled up in front of them were stacks of crockery, linen, clothing, as though they had just moved in (though that had been half a year ago), and at last we entered the fifth room, the engine room as Katharina called it. *The engine room*—a name that seemed to me too coarse for the machines kept there.

The room was panelled right up to the ceiling. The machines stood on slender pedestals, under bell jars, others on low tables, some on the floor in front of the wooden crates they had been packed in. She told me, in her quiet, languid voice, giving every syllable equal weight, that these were mechanical calculators, that long before Hollerith built his first machine, these could carry out the four basic operations in arithmetic—plus and minus, times and divide—with their drums, cogs and levers. Her father had assembled this collection and the oldest piece was from 1709, built by the Italian Poleni—a name that came back to me as I walked along the bank and that I have not forgotten to this day. *Poleni, Poleni.* She was Swiss but spoke without the slightest trace of an accent or of dialect. The only thing you noticed was that she would pause slightly between words, as though remembering grammatical rules or usage. *Come*! And then we went up the stairs, to her room, where she opened the drawer and took out lighter, needle and ink.

The bus went under the S-Bahn bridge, the lock lay to our left, the land beyond it partly allotment gardens, partly wasteland, ruined by war or the collapse of industries, by subsidence or bankruptcy, weeds, nettles, trees overshadowing it all and after that a tangle of roads and motorway exits, a black skull-and-crossbones flag flying in a garden. Early evening, July or August, but I remember that there was already something autumnal about the light, that light where every object takes on sharp lines. The woman put her hand in her bag (the movement reflected in the window), took out a sheet of paper and smoothed it out. The notepaper she had written on as I watched through the window?

The bus left the clearway and after the motorway bridge it turned onto the roundabout that leads to the airport, last stop. We stood up, the doors opened with a cough, we got out, she went toward the large revolving door but then changed her mind and took the next door, I followed her. In the hall she glanced at the board above the passage to the low-cost agencies, where I could see the foot of an escalator at the end. She looked at the clock, the hands stood just past seven. Was she here to meet someone? Had someone given her a landing time, as I stood there and watched? Three-quarters of an hour had passed since the telephone call. Four red lights glowed on the indicator board, four planes landed, two delayed, three due in the next half hour. We passed a bistro and the smell of coffee wafted over.

Now she was walking more quickly and still moved in that smooth, gliding way and still had that air of stillness that had surrounded Katharina like a cocoon, like an armoured shell which deflected everything, so that my grandfather called her aloof. He would say she's aloof. She's not there half the time. She's a dark one. Say? No, but he made it clear enough that's what he thought when he spoke instead about Katharina's friend Rita, calling her 'a girl with heart'. He had kind words to say about one but when he heard me mention the other he would make a worried face, to tell me that he would rather I had feelings for the girl with heart.

Rita was the daughter of the high-street shoe-shop owner, known to all, while hardly anyone had ever seen Katharina's father. He seemed to avoid mixing with the townsfolk. In those days the only foreigners we ever saw were the Italians who ran the Dolomite ice-cream parlour and the Dutch, who drove south past us in their camper vans. So her father's remoteness gave rise to all sorts of speculation, about foreigners in general and about this one in particular—gossip that made him out to be a retired diplomat, a professor emeritus, a general, a swindler who had made his fortune in murky deals and was hiding it from the Swiss police in our town. While all these stories circulated, I was only surprised by how old he was.

Katharina was seventeen but he must have been over ninety and could have been her great-grandfather while his wife could easily be mistaken for Katharina's sister. The same cast of features, the same colour hair, the same figure, the same unruffled way of walking. In the spring she was sometimes seen on the cafe terrace by the water tower, leafing through a glossy magazine, and as summer drew on was spotted in the restaurant at the station, where she would order nothing to eat but a cognac, sit for a while, brooding over the glass, and finally ask for a telephone. To her table? Yes. But there was no such thing as telephones to the table and so every time she would wrangle for a moment, then go to the corner between the bar and the toilets—people said that they heard her speaking French or Spanish, though others said Portuguese, into the receiver.

Odd? Perhaps. But it did not bother me. Because unlike the shoe-shop owner's daughter, the girl my grandfather preferred, the daughter of this lady (with her mysterious telephone calls) was serenely beautiful, well-proportioned in body, limbs and face. My grandfather distrusted her but her beauty was the sort that had an effect even on those less favoured. How else can I explain why Rita followed her like a faithful dog? She never left her side within the school gates and in the afternoons we saw her standing, until evening drew in, by the fence of the red-brick villa, gazing longingly at the windows, half hidden by the trees. Only the dogs patrolling the garden stopped her from setting foot in the grounds, to be nearer to her friend.

She had some defect in the bones of her legs and with every step she took, her body lurched back and forth like a ship in a storm. She could only walk with difficulty and yet, every morning, she rocked and wobbled her way halfway across town to meet Katharina at home. She would wait at the gates until she came out, then walk swaying at her side all the way to school for no other reward than to be seen with her. She talked to her in a hissing, lisping voice and when I joined them she would fall silent and glare furiously at me. She wanted to be left alone with her princess and saw anyone who dared disturb their time together as an enemy. If she was at all a girl with heart, as my grandfather said, the heart had been buried under this ridiculous love—and all the while, the object of her affection seemed not to notice.

Rita's overtures simply glanced off Katharina. She neither rejected them nor gave a single word, a glance or gesture that might acknowledge them. She kept her counsel, equally distant from anything and anyone and this did not discourage Rita but rather spurred her on to ever greater shows of affection. Once I heard her whisper some words not meant for my ears, inviting her lady love to a rock concert—she had got hold of two almost unobtainable tickets. Another time I heard a rustling sound and when I looked over I saw that she had taken an expensive fountain pen from her bag. Still in its presentation case, it lay on her open hand, wobbling back and forth because of that unfortunate disability. Both of these gifts, the concert tickets and the pen, were refused with a barely perceptible shake of the head.

The road we took to school sloped upwards in the final stretch. Katharina walked in the middle, Rita on the left, lurching, whispering, hissing, myself on the right, trapped in a clumsy body in which everything seemed thumbs and elbows, while Katharina glided between us, serene, indifferently friendly.

The woman who looked like Katharina turned into the passage that led to the gates. To our right, a little lower down was the car park. The sun stood low over the roof of the round building, the roofs of the cars showed through the glass frontage. To our left, the desks, departures and arrivals next to one another. It was busier here than it had been on the concourse, people approaching us with bags and suitcases, luggage trolleys, children running round. But her cocoon seemed to work like some kind of wedge that split the crowd in front of her. People swerved aside, opened up a path for her. She walked briskly ahead while I had to dodge my way round the people, the trolleys, the children, always finding someone standing in my way, walking a zigzag course while she seemed to glide forward on wheels.

The crowd grew thicker in front of the Air France desk, a throng of people, cheek by jowl. In front of the desk? No, at the barrier in front of the frosted glass, the door where the passengers would emerge. A woman held a rose with silver paper wrapped round the stem, a child sat on a man's shoulders among a cluster of balloons. A black dog wearing a muzzle and kept on a short leash growled low and loud. And at that moment I saw myself again, on that morning by the canal path, my hand under my shirt—trying to reach where it burnt.

The path along the bank, the jetty, the skirt of reeds, the water where the pike lurk and, suddenly, as I stood there, the barking, the dogs barking furiously, having torn free of Katharina's grip—I knew straightaway—and rushed down the driveway. Now they were on my trail. The barking tore through the morning silence in the streets of the town, came nearer and when I thought that the dogs were about to appear on the canal path, I climbed a fence so that I could keep moving inside the gardens. Raspberry canes, gooseberry bushes, green potatoes that had been lifted too early, stunted plum and peach trees hung with scattered fruit, a rain barrel half-full, the reflection of the sun, just risen, in the window panes of a low block of flats.

The gardens abutted one another, I climbed fence after fence and finally reached my grandfather's garden. The whole time I could hear the dogs barking, very close, as though they were coming along the canal path, then further away, as though they were still running down the street, but the noise was there the whole time and only fell silent—as though someone had turned off a switch—the moment I went into the house.

My grandfather was still asleep. My memory tells me that I climbed the stairs to my room unobserved, went to bed and then lay awake for a long time. The spot on my back burnt and when I shut my eyes I saw Katharina on the bed, her back, then saw her standing there, her heels dug in, her shoulder and the strap that had slipped from it, her arms naked, the dogs tearing at their collars. *Now go!* I heard her say it again, *Now go!* and this time too—I remember—she put a tiny pause between the words. And didn't I see a movement at the window when I turned round one last time at the gates? Yes, now that I lay there on the bed, I was sure that I had seen her mother's face in the bow window above the door. Below, at the foot of the steps, the girl with the dogs, and above her on the first floor her mother's face, so like hers that for a moment I thought I saw two Katharinas.

The woman who looked like Katharina (or should I say, her double?) had stopped. She was standing among the crowd, studying the board. The plane from Lyon was ten minutes late. She glided through the crowd and sat down on a radiator cover in front of the glass wall. She leant back on her hands and looked round and when our eyes met I thought I saw irony there, something ironic in her gaze, as though she had recognized me—the man from the travel agency—or as though she knew that I was following her, a flash of irony, no, not a flash, but a long ironic stare, before she turned her head to the side with the same movement that Katharina had used that morning, when she said, *Now go!*

A small crease had formed between her eyes and her pupils had narrowed almost imperceptibly—an ironic gaze, beyond question, and at the time I had thought that it was mockery, mockery of my foolishness, my inexperience, my fear of the dogs, though today I think something else. Today I think that at that moment she already knew how that day would end. She knew that I would hurry down the driveway, turn round one last time at the bottom and see her mother's face, that after crossing all the gardens I would lie awake, thinking of her, then fall asleep after all and be woken by Rita's voice on Sunday at noon. She already knew. She foresaw it. And I think that it was part of her plan, just as it had been part of her plan to walk along the canal with me the evening before, Saturday evening, as dusk fell, to sit on the bank—all of this wordlessly, all with various tendernesses—holding hands, squeezing hands, embraces that were not rebuffed, that were returned, open-mouthed kisses and her tongue darting in and out, running my hands all over her body (she was wearing a thin dress, my hand ran across it, over her back, her buttocks, her legs, and felt every muscle, every sinew)—at first under the willows by the bank, then, as we walked through town, in doorways, and part of her plan to lead me at last up the driveway, through the rooms of the villa—*Poleni, Poleni*—and then to climb the stairs.

I was leaning against the wall of a grey office cabin that stuck out into the passage, across from the Air France exit, when all of a sudden a movement ran through the crowd. They surged forward and when I looked at the indicator board I saw that the plane had landed, the little lamp was lit. The woman who looked like Katharina (or her double) stood up but stayed where she was by the glass wall, even when the passengers came through the sliding doors. I looked from her to the doors and back again, her face was quite still. At last she left her spot and glided through the crowd—now I would see who she had been waiting for—but instead of heading for anyone, she turned toward the concourse and once we were there I saw that she was following someone. I followed her and she followed a man I could see only from behind. He was wearing a green polo shirt and light trousers, a flight bag hung over his shoulder. His neck was tanned, his hair trimmed short. Outside, he looked around and then went across to the taxis, the driver got out, took his bag and put it into the boot, while the man took his seat in the back.

She had followed him but stopped by the revolving door. I was standing inside, behind the glass, watching her watch the taxi. Meanwhile the driver had got in too. The car started up and when the man on the back seat turned his head to face us, I saw myself, my face. I saw myself driving away in the taxi and I ran outside, but it had already turned into the clearway. I stood behind her, looking at the car, and then she turned round and asked if I would go with her. No, I will try to give her exact words. They seemed to me important and I have gone over them again and again since then. As if she knew that I was standing there, she turned round and said, 'Since we know one another, I want to ask if you would keep me company.' Not *go with her*, not in those terms. *Since we know one another*. Do you say that to someone you have seen only once? *I want to ask*. When she spoke her voice was not like it had been in the travel agency. She had a languid tone.

'Now?'

'If you don't mind.'

Yes, this was the same languid voice, giving every syllable equal weight. I looked down at the place on her blouse where she had taken off the name badge and I saw the marks of the pin, two tiny points left behind where the badge had been. She turned back to the concourse, I walked along beside her, so close that I could catch a breath of her perfume before it was masked by the smell of coffee. Coffee was the predominant smell here in the concourse, just as the concourse itself looked less like an airport space than the main strip of a mall, with shop lined up after shop, interrupted by bistros and cafes.

She was not walking fast, but nevertheless, I found that I had trouble keeping up with her. My legs felt heavy. It was as though the old clumsiness had returned, the awkward manner, the tendency to trip, so that all my concentration went on not falling over. She aimed toward the upright tables across from the large indicator board but then hurried past these into the cafe and settled on one of the sofas. I plumped down into a chair opposite her, crossed my legs, immediately regretted doing so (my trousers pinched at the groin) but stayed sitting as I was, for fear that if I uncrossed my legs I could well overturn the table.

We were silent. The waiter came. I ordered a café au lait, she asked for water. He brought both. The bottle was blue, skittle-shaped. Next to my coffee cup lay a biscuit wrapped in cellophane and as I tore it open, she asked whether I know it—her voice dark, languid, her posture upright but unforced, her face still, but not motionless, rather, lost in thought, her movements so discreet that you only noticed them when she stopped moving. I never once heard her put down the glass while my coffee cup rattled against the saucer every time.— Do I know it.—What?—The burning. Suddenly, years after-wards, to find yourself thinking of someone obsessively, imagining how they would look today, wanting to ask them one or two things that you could never discuss back then, and then in the moment when you could speak, not making yourself known. She gazed out into the concourse.

Here I am. I wanted to say, 'Here I am,' then realized that she was talking about the other man and as I thought of him, I found that I was dizzy. My face behind the taxi window, and at the same time I saw Katharina sitting opposite me, the same woman. That was what she had wanted to tell me, she said, which was easy enough for her since she knew that I would forget everything, this meeting, her words, by tomor-row I would have forgotten everything. And she picked up her bag. I asked whether I could see her again (hurriedly, for she was already on her feet).—Certainly.—Where?—Did I know the cafe in the Schlossstrasse, she asked. The one with the garden.—But of course.—Good then. Till this evening.— And as I waved to the waiter, she had already left between the tables.

But she did not come.

Moreover, the dizziness lasted for hours and as I sat there under the canopy of leaves in the garden cafe, my shoulder burnt too, a strong pain to match the disorientation. By tomorrow. I was writing fast, noting down everything, for I did not think she had chosen those words at random, *by tomorrow*, no more than I thought she had not foreseen everything, including the trouble with the dogs. Including Rita shouting up at my window on Sunday at noon.

I was still asleep. Her voice screeched like a saw blade stuck in a plank and in the pauses my grandfather's voice as he tried to calm her. A moment's silence, then Rita squealing again, she was walking round the house and shouting at me that I was to blame, guilty, it was my fault that the dogs had torn Katharina to pieces. This was what she had foreseen, that Rita would bring the news about her and the dogs and that I would leap out of bed and run to the brick villa.

Rita lurched along next to me, repeating like a litany what she had heard from a man. As she was about to take her place at the fence as she did every Sunday, a man had stepped out from the bushes and had told her that he had seen a boy coming down the driveway that morning and when he looked up the drive he had seen two dogs tearing a girl to pieces. She repeated this all the way there. When I asked who the man was, though, and what he had done to save the girl, she couldn't tell me. I asked whether she knew the man. No, but she saw that he was very old. And at once I suspected that things were very different from what I had feared, from what Rita believed. (My suspicions were confirmed that evening. When I went to the hospital and explained things to a doctor, he said, 'My dear young fellow, when someone suffers fatal dog bites, he's sent to us even if it's just to help the police investigation along. Since that hasn't happened, I advise you to go back home and stop worrying.')

It is true that the dogs were lying on the driveway. As we came up the drive, we saw them lying in a puddle of dried blood, with flies swarming above them. And we wondered who had shot them, for it was easy to see that they had been shot from the perfectly round holes above their eyes. They lay next to one another, roughly where Katharina had been holding them, meaning, not far from the door under the five-pointed star with the G in the middle.

The door was shut but not locked. Rita called up to the windows and when there was no answer, we went in, and as we went through the rooms we saw that the furniture had all been taken away. The panelled room was empty, the mechanical calculators that had been standing on pedestals, on tables, on the floor, had vanished along with their crates. The stacks of crockery were likewise gone, the heaps of clothes and even the wardrobes. Nothing was left behind. While I was asleep, the pantechnicons had come. Or whatever such people use to move house.

When I sat there under the leafy canopy of the garden cafe and began to write, I had taken my watch off and put it next to the notepad, keeping the hands in sight, *by tomorrow, tomorrow*, and at half past eleven I put the cap back on the pen and shut the notepad. From now on I would only be able to remember with the help of those words I had written, while everything else, even this moment, would be consigned to oblivion. I sat there for a little while, then got up and went out into the street.

It was about half past midnight. I saw the palace—it is lit up at night—between the trees on the avenue, looking like a stage set from this distance. It only starts to look like a real building as you approach but tonight it still looked like painted scenery even as I came closer. My shoulder burnt. Written in my notepad were the words 'Do I know it.' I knew it all. Those had been my questions that she asked while I simply sat there like a block of wood and when she sailed away I did not get up and run after her, grab hold of her, but sat where I was. Potted palm trees and agaves stood in front of the pavilion, throwing artificial shadows in the stage-like light and all of a sudden, I recalled the article I had read a few weeks after she had disappeared. When I got home from school the newspaper was lying on the table. My grandfather had folded the pages back so that I could not miss the news.

During an auction at Christie's in London, an absurd sort of duel had broken out between two bidders. One of them, described as a mystery man, was sitting in the auction hall, while the other was a collector from Zurich, bidding via telephone. The lot was a mechanical calculator built by the German Johann Christoph Schuster in 1822, valued by the experts at thirty thousand pounds, yet, within a few minutes the price had reached astronomical heights, twenty million pounds. Neither bidder wanted to back down and their behaviour left observers baffled. And at last, the man from Zurich had won the bidding.

Having read that far, I thought I knew whom the story was about, there was no doubt, I decided, it was her father, they had moved back to Switzerland, but as I read on I saw that I was wrong. Once the man in Zurich had won the bid, the other had left the hall straightaway but that same evening a young lady appeared at Christie's in a state of some excitement and handed over a business card on behalf of the losing bidder. On one side was an address in Cornwall, on other the words, 'Just in case'.

At first the staff at Christie's didn't know what to make of it. Then two days later, the collector in Zurich called them, desperate, confessing that he had no way of raising the twenty million pounds and saw no way out of the situation but to turn for help to the unknown man whose intransigence had ruined him. In return for the amount of the final bid, he was ready to let him have not just the Schuster machine but his entire collection, about twenty-six of the most famous mechanical calculators in existence.

Cornwall then, not Zurich. They had moved to England. For days afterwards, I could see her gliding through a landscape of rolling hills, headed for a Tudor mansion, where the crates of mechanical calculators were just being delivered, while the dogs, other dogs, barked furiously. She would speak English as if to the manner born but with a languid intonation, and at some point she would have my doppelgänger in her room and show him lighter, candle, needle and ink, while out in the garden the dogs already ran.

I stopped on the bridge behind the pavilion, thinking that I had heard a noise. The lights wreathed round the bridge spans had been switched off and there was hardly any traffic on the streets. Yes, a noise, the soft thrumming of a good-sized boat, not coming and not leaving, but tied up somewhere upstream. Back at my flat I went to the window, and at that moment I saw a boat cruise by at full speed. An S-class boat, which, strictly speaking, should not be navigating these shallow, narrow waters. The wheelhouse was dark, but the halls, cabins and walkways were lit up as bright as day, as though for a party for which the guests had failed to turn up—there was no one to be seen on the boat. It glided past and I read the name on the stern, *Katharina*, whereupon I opened my notepad again and wrote down what I had seen.

seven

ZERO FORTY

The trickles running through the garden are spreading out wider by the hour, the ditches along the sides of the fields have already passed their brief moment as streams and are now swollen into aimless rivers, joining those shown on the maps (the ordinary rivers) or seeking the sea on their own. I am surrounded by rivers as though they followed me when I fled from them. Once there was a man who brought the desert with him wherever he went, the grass died under his very feet. In my case, rivers bubble up. The hawk in the apple tree droops his wings and if the cat can even make it past the front door, she squats disconsolately in the porch. The only creatures who feel happy in this weather are the snails, who are breeding so extraordinarily fast and producing such fine fat offspring that it beggars belief. They are almost the size of saucers and creep about leaving cross-cross quicksilver trails over the sodden paths and the walls. If you don't shut the door as soon as you leave, three of them will be sitting on the threshold and heading into the house, where everything made of cloth has picked up a musty odour by now, the clothes are all damp and the wood seems to be rotting. Moisture has seeped into every nook and cranny and when I switch on the laptop, the first thing I see is a crosshatched pattern, lines like rain in front of a deep night-blue, lines seeping along from top right to bottom left, precipitation even in this little electronic box of tricks, as though to show that we are in an age of worldwide downpours. Whenever I log in to see what's going on in the world, the stripes are there to greet me, and only then does the screen switch to *send message/ receive.*

Zero forty. What is that? A measurement? A year? A time? For two days now, every time the crosshatched rain fades from my screen, I receive a message saying *Zero forty*, anonymous, no sender ID, some nameless and unidentified person is sending me *Zero forty*. But he keeps me in the dark as to why. Is this rain to fall for forty days? Will the water reach this level (but what's the unit of measurement?)? Is it an information, a warning, a promise? Is someone announcing a visit at zero forty hours? Or will someone be sitting in a bar somewhere at zero forty hours and waiting for me to appear? Or has someone already sat there, without my coming? Is the message meant to remind me of what I have failed to do? Isn't this the time when I go out at night once more, along the asphalted paths?

No railway lines far and wide? True. But once, many years ago, there was one. Not for passengers or tourists but, rather, for the potash salts ripped from the earth here in the first quarter of the last century, that had to be transported somehow, so that an embankment was built between the mine (close to the village) and the nearest main line junction—a causeway that runs straight as an arrow across the fields—where they laid the sleepers and rails and where a company locomotive pulled the mine trucks back and forth, so that the rattle of their wheels could be heard for miles around, iron on iron, day and night, summer and winter, until the deposits were worked out and the sound of the wheels died away. The potash company recalled its engineers and technicians, and the farmers' sons who had been recruited locally, made into miners for a while, went back to their fields.

All this a long time ago but the memory of these glorious years of progress and prosperity has endured. Even after the now-useless rails were taken up and the railway became a country greenway, people still call it the old mine track. The buildings over the shafts have all subsided and are overgrown with twisted trees and scrub, crumbling stumps of walls rear out of the tall grass, rusty barbed wire and iron fence posts (the grass is flattened by the rain by now) and here and there holes yawn, their edges overgrown, sudden fathomless pits leading down into the depths. And in the middle of this tangle of growth and the sinkholes, a perfectly round lake, like an eye staring up into the sky, where the shafts collapsed. Even today, eighty years later, two heaps of pure potassium salts stand not far from the embankment, tall as houses, shining as white as Kilimanjaro when they are dry but now turned mouse-grey or black with the prevailing weather.

The paths I take to walk at night are flooded, so now I turn my steps the other way, away from the asphalt paths, past the defunct tavern, along hedges and fences, until the potash heaps rear up just past the copse, a well-watered meadow, and then the strip of asphalt lined on either side by low trees that grow aslant, leaning away from the constant wind—this is where the mine trucks ran and now the rain drives across, on this side of the river the fields look like lakes. Up ahead a light, shining over the water to the left. Obviously the village has sent people out, walking now with lanterns along this greenway, higher than the surrounding land, the last connection to the outside world.

The washed-out light sweeps over the water and is immediately switched off. A shout rings out, more like a birdcall than a human voice, warbling uncertainly over the embankment. It passes over my head and once it dies away, I hear someone next to me, so close that I think I could touch him. Is someone there? One of the men sent out to keep watch? I hear his footsteps, slapping and shuffling, and I turn to one side but in this blackness, this saturated air, I can't even see the trees at the edge of the track that slant upward into the sky, it is as though someone had pulled a hood over my head.

I think that I'm standing in the middle of the track, yes, there's someone there, and I stretch out my hand but my hand closes on emptiness, and now all of a sudden, as I stand there, I notice that it was the echo of my own footsteps, for all at once the slapping and shuffling has stopped. Or has the someone else stopped moving too? I hold my breath, listen hard. No. No one. And now I hear the roar of the rain as well, roaring down without pause, just like the night—early eighties, in the south-easternmost corner of Poland—when I charged up the steps to the railway line.

Was that at zero hours forty? Certainly it was after midnight, for at midnight I was still sitting in the bar where we were to meet, keeping an eye on the clock above the door, the rain drumming against the window and out on the street the truck tyres singing and whooshing, splashing water against the front wall, and every time the girl behind the bar (I think she was washing glasses) glanced at me accusingly: He should leave! I want to close. When's he going? But I couldn't, I had to wait. If I had left, we might have missed one another and if we missed one another—how would the woman who wanted to come with us get past the guards? Even if you didn't see them, they were there nonetheless, leaning motionless against the barrack walls, smoking, cupping the cigarette in their hand, hiding the glow, keeping a sharp eye on the gate and the barrier. And even if she had managed to give them the slip, she would never have found the quay in this labyrinth of branching canals, warehouses, silos and coal heaps, not in this darkness, not in this rain.

'At eleven o'clock. Eleven, at the bar.'

No, this was the place and I had to wait. If she had come at eleven, we could have sailed at twelve. I was counting on twenty minutes on foot, that's to say it was twenty minutes to the gate but she didn't have a pass, so that it was not advisable to go anywhere near the gate. There was a road running along the fence and a thin wooded strip next to this. The fence was lit up as bright as day but one of the searchlights had failed further up—there, that was the place. We would have to walk along the road through the woods, with the rustling and the cracking underfoot, and when we reach the dark spot, cross the road, then I could, perhaps, cut a hole in the wire mesh. At eleven. But eleven was long past, as was twelve. We would have to cast off at one o'clock at the latest, since customs was already on board and had sealed the cargo.

Now I can see the clock again, its hands trembling as they ticked onward and I hear how the glasses clink together as the girl puts them back on the racks—is she tired? does she do it deliberately?—so that each one chimes. At last, as the chimes sounded, the door opened, I leapt to my feet and then sat down again, since the person who came in, shoving aside the curtain that hung before the door to stop the wind, was not her but a man, middling height, long hair dripping with rain. He wore a heavy jacket like mine (that's to say, mine hung over the back of the chair) and stamped his feet so hard that drops of water sprayed out everywhere, as when a dog shakes itself.

After looking about, he came toward me, leaving a trail of water behind him, unfastened the lowest button of his jacket and said my name. A police check? No. It was not my real name, rather, unexpectedly, he called me by a name from my childhood, a nickname that my grandfather had made up, a name no one here knew—in this country, in this town on the upper reaches of the river, almost in the mountains, with its port where the ships barely put in, where I had never been before. No one? No, there was one person who knew it, one woman. I had let slip the name as we lay together one night on the bed in the warehouse. Had she remembered it and passed it on to this rain-soaked stranger, as proof that he came from her, that I could trust him? Was it a password? Water dripped from his hair down his brow and he wiped it away with his hand, and as he did so I saw a tattoo on his forearm, about the size of a fingernail. I think it showed a rose and he said, 'Is that you? I'm to tell you then, there's been a change of plan.' He fell silent, probably to see how I would react but I moved not a muscle and he carried on, irked or possibly simply wanting to get it over and done with, 'She can't come, she's waiting at the railway station.'

'And?'

'If you like, I can take you along.'

'Is it far?'

'I have a motorbike.'

The minute hand ticked forward to twenty minutes after twelve, zero hours twenty. One o'clock at the latest—I looked across at the girl, but she had dropped her cloth as soon as the man came in dripping water and had gone through the door behind the bar. I called but she stayed out of sight, so I took a banknote from my wallet that was probably worth several times the bill and put it under my cup. He nodded curtly as I did so and I knew then that he saw his opinion of foreigners confirmed . . . they change their currency into our zloty, we force them to take it and then they throw it away to show us how little they think of it. But what was I supposed to do if the girl wouldn't come? As I put on my jacket, the wire cutters almost fell out of my pocket, slipping forward so that I grabbed to catch them. Luckily he had turned round at that moment and gone to the windbreak. He drew the heavy curtain aside, opened the door (through which I could see the rain like a second curtain) and as I went past him I could smell his breath, he had been drinking and now I remember that only then I wondered what his relationship to her might be. Was he family? A colleague?

'What is it?'

He stood there in the pouring rain next to the motorbike, which was not up on its rest but simply leaning against the wall of the bar. Indeed, now I recall that it was leaning on the wall because it had no stand that could be folded down, it was an older model. He kicked the starter pedal until the engine howled, swung himself onto the saddle and hardly had I sat down—I was still looking for the footrests—than he roared away, so that I would have been flung off if I had not grabbed his jacket, then flung my arms round his chest—

there was no passenger grab handle either—and clung to his back and we sped up the street, sheathed in the downpour and in water splashing up from the road surface.

Those houses we passed (there hardly were any) were dark and as we approached a slope on the left he turned his head and shouted something in his language, a sibilant concatenation of sounds, a long hissing word or perhaps a number of words together and when I saw his face, eyeball to eyeball with mine, I knew that he could happily kill me. And involuntarily my arm grabbed him even more tightly, while my other hand felt for the wire cutters and as though he had read my thoughts he began to laugh and shoved his right foot down so hard on the accelerator that the bike leapt forward as if from a standing start—though we were moving already, and fast.

Meanwhile, we had left the houses behind, but the slope still lay to our left, while meadows stretched out on the right with trees standing clumped here and there. Were these the trees we went to when we once met, not by night at the warehouse gates, but in daylight, at the town gates? Isn't this where we saw cranes in the distance that marked the port? My eyes tried to find the horizon but in this dark, in this rain. He braked suddenly and when we stopped he pointed to steps leading up the slope a little way ahead. We were both still sitting on the motorbike but he was in front of me and my hand was in my pocket, on the handle of the wire cutters.

'Up there, she's waiting up there.'

And indeed, I could see a roof, now, silhouetted at the top of the slope and hear the rumble of wheels. I listened hard. The rumbling wheels became louder, stronger, and wasn't that a movement up at the top of the steps? Yes, there was someone standing there, hunched against the rain, half lit up by the floodlights that blazed through the darkness without themselves being seen (the light was like a wall). I took my hand from my pocket and ran for the steps, and as I reached them, I heard him panting hoarsely behind me, first that sibilant word, then, 'Stop! There's something I want to know.' But I ran on, the wheels screeching above me, a train stopping. Was it stopping? I couldn't see anything, only the steps leading steeply upwards, and I leapt up the steps, he was behind me, his hand (was it his hand?) tangled my foot, something tripped me, I fell, and now I could feel his weight, his knee in my back.

'Did you fuck her?' he shouted. 'Did you fuck her?'

He dragged me to my feet. The next thing I heard was the roar of the motorbike moving away. Was I . . . had he slammed my head against the steps? I don't know but I know that I stood and ran up the steps. Or am I wrong? Did I actually stay lying where I was . . . lying there until they came with their torch, grabbed my arms and legs, and threw me like a sack of potatoes onto the flatbed of a truck parked at the bottom of the steps? But if I never made it to the station platform . . . where do I get that image from—the two men walking toward a train that shunts out clouds of steam, who fling back the door and then shove the woman into the carriage? Until then, she was hidden between them, but now they shut the door after her. And the image of a clock, its hands ticking forward to zero forty hours at the very moment the train moves off?

If I was there at all, I was too far away. I should have gone closer. Although I was there, I surely saw it, I remember only outlines, a movement, a yanking and shoving motion, barely visible in the darkness, in the rain that was still pouring down when the truck stopped at the barrier and the guards came strolling toward us, throwing away their cigarettes.

eight

THE MISTAKE

Up ahead, at the end of the mine track, is the town where I
spent my first night hereabouts, a small place that lost any
significance it ever had once the potash era was over. I only
reached it in the evening, after many hours on the bus. Everything about the place made such a desolate first impression
that I looked yearningly after the bus lights as it disappeared
round the bend. There was not a soul on the streets although
it was only just after six o'clock. Wasn't this the time of day
when people bustle home with their shopping? But here? The
blinds were let down on ground-floor windows where heavy
curtains hung, the sort that stop those outside seeing in and
those inside seeing out, and the houses themselves looked as
though they only stayed upright thanks to the posts stuck in
the ground to prop up their roofs. A bridge leading over a
stream and a single street, half ripped up, squeezed together,
was called the *Historic town centre* on an ornately carved
wooden signpost. Even more depressing was the newly built
town enclosing these, single-storey L-shaped bungalows and
storey-and-a-half properties with the extra flats shoehorned
in to cut down on residential tax, all these barricaded behind
rustic fences, flowerbeds and neatly kept lawns. I dragged my
wheeled suitcase through the deserted streets and inside the

suitcase my laptop, while the wind blustered in my face and the street lamps swayed.

An abandoned farmhouse, well no, there was no way that the house I was looking for was here, so I went back into the historic centre, which impressed me so little that even the lit facade of a drugstore would have been a welcome sight or an unlit hotel sign. And indeed there was a hotel or a *pension* or some such, the door swinging creaking back when I turned the handle. A heavyset woman of indeterminate age got up from a bench, grumbling. She had a flat sort of face, typical— though I did not know this yet, I was soon to find out—for the squat breed often seen hereabouts, and she shuffled behind the reception desk.

'Pardon me.'

I dug out the sheet of paper although I knew the address by heart. The landlady, which is what she was, took the sheet in both hands, held it close to her eyes, gave it back to me and said, 'Huh, that's about ten kilometres.'

'As far as that?'

'Not 'ny closer, no.'

'Is there a bus?'

'In the morning.'

'A taxi?'

She nodded. Yes, but it would have to be called to come from the next large town and if it came at all (here she sighed) it would be hours late. Not that I believed her. Hadn't the man I rented from said, 'The village is near . . .' But suddenly I was tired and thought, the house, empty, unheated. Did I have to reach there today? No, I could just as well stay here. And I asked the landlady for a room.

As she led me up the stairs, her hands swept automatically, incessantly, up and down her skirt, leaving a greasy sheen behind on the fabric (on the hips). She wore brown surgical stockings which kept the flesh from bursting out. In the night, looking for the toilet, I heard groans echoing through the hallways, not the panting of two lovers but one person's moans, a boy's, tugging with his hand as he bent over a magazine. The door had sprung from the latch, so that I could see into his room, the bedside light burnt, he sat in bed, his trousers bunched at his feet, one hand on the magazine, the other frigging between his legs, and when he looked up I went on, onwards into the smell of camphor that flooded out from another room, its door likewise open, yes, it must have been camphor that the landlady used as embrocation. She squirted something onto the palm of her hand and kneaded it into the flesh she had freed from her stockings, unhealthily white under the light of the ceiling lamp.

And when I came back to my room I saw zero forty on the digital clock on the bedside table. At that moment there was a clack and the hand ticked forward, a noise that came every minute, enough to drive you mad—a Chinese torture, clack, or a headsman's sword somewhere in the clockwork, clack, that chopped away minute after minute from my life, just now you had this long, clack, now only . . . with every leap of the clock hands and every clack, life became shorter, and I lay in this hotel, in this room, in this bed, and somewhere, unreachable, were cities, conversations, railway stations, trains, ports, rivers, boats passing. The wind shoved at the window, and then I got dressed, left the money on the bedside table, took my suitcase and went to the stairs, in the dark, quietly, so that the two of them would not hear me—

their doors were closed now. But when I came downstairs, the boy (yes, him) stepped forward from a corner as though he had been waiting for me and gestured with his hands. A thin light came through the window over the door, down to his shoulders. 'What is it?' I said. He stepped forward, vanishing in darkness once more. 'You really going?' I heard his voice in my ear. 'Why won't you stay?' And when I said, 'I can't,' he whispered that in that case, he was coming with me.

Before I could reply he leapt to the door, turned the key and went in front of me out onto the street. The lamps had switched off, a white sickle moon shone, clouds scurried across the sky. The boy was about my height but so thin that his jumper flapped and gusted like an empty potato sack when the wind caught it. He had turned the ends of the sleeves inside themselves and pulled them down over the backs of his hands. Despite the flat nose and pouting lips, his face was not unattractive.

'Listen, young man,' I said, keeping a formal tone (for I had found his words much too familiar) while I put the suitcase onto its wheels, having carried it out of the building hoping not to be heard, 'If it's about the money, that's under the clock on the bedside table.' 'But I'm not gonna take money from you,' he said, thrusting his lower lip out. Was he offended? Why? And all of a sudden I felt doubts. 'You are from the hotel, aren't you?' He shook his head, as though taken aback by my obtuseness, and answered, smiling, 'The landlady's my mother.' 'Well then,' I said, 'the room's been paid for, if that's what it is.' And I walked on down the narrow, bumpy pavement, he trotting alongside me on the street, arms wrapped about himself, turning his toes in as he walked (he was wearing plimsolls).

'Listen,' I said again. 'If you are coming with me anyway, you could perhaps show me how to get to the mine track.' I suddenly remembered the name that the man who rented the place to me had used—the old mine track. 'The village is at the end of the mine track.' Ten kilometres? If I kept up a good pace, I could reach the house by daybreak. The boy looked at me. 'But why? It doesn't lead anywhere but one of the villages.' I kept quiet. Or perhaps I shrugged my shoulders, whereupon he sighed. 'The mine track. We've got to go this way.'

He stepped up onto the pavement and herded me onto a street that indeed led, after it had narrowed one last time, out of the tangle of houses and twittens, a sports field fringed with poplars, paddocks, then we turned and were walking on an avenue that ran straight as an arrow, with bushes to the left and right, then trees and behind these—below us, for the avenue was on an embankment—fields stretched away. 'The potash track?' He nodded. I thought that now he would turn round but he stayed, stayed at my side, and now I heard him say, still in that familiar tone, 'Where've you been all this time?' And although that had nothing to do with him—what kind of impertinence was this?—and I did not intend to reply, I saw before me all the cities where I had lived, all the rivers, ports and boats. 'Ach,' I said and huddled down before the wind that gusted with fresh strength. The boy's jumper filled like a sail.

For a while all I could hear was the whistle of the wind as it scoured the fields and the hum and whirr of the wheels on my suitcase, our footsteps, or rather, my own, since he walked noiselessly in those soft shoes, then at last he cleared his throat. 'You don't want to talk about it? Pity. But I want to tell you that I'm happy you're here.' There was a bridge ahead of us, crossing a stream fed from the ditches around these fields, and once we reached the bridge I stopped and said, 'I think you should turn back now.' He looked up (yes, he was a little shorter than me) and now I saw his eyes, staring at me in surprise, no, in hatred, 'You're sending me away?' for a brief moment before the mild gaze returned. He shook his head. 'No,' then, more to himself than to me, 'Now that you're here, I'll stay.'

'Would you care to tell me what exactly you mean by that?'

'You were away so long.'

Nonsense. But now I knew that I had to be on my guard. His eyes.

I grasped hold of my suitcase handle, walked on. The moon had vanished but the clouds scudded across the sky, harbingers of the rain that would soon fall. Up ahead the dawn crept in and as on my journey here I saw windmills, their three-armed shapes scattered across the whole landscape. And just as I thought that the boy had stayed behind after all—I couldn't see him and didn't want to turn round—I heard him behind me, so close that I felt his breath on my neck, my nape. 'You've got to understand.' Then, alongside me once more, 'I don't know anything about you and I should know all there is to know.' Was he mad? If so, how exactly? Was he a simpleton, a harmless chatterbox, or was he the dangerous sort of madman? I put my hand into my pocket and took hold of the key that my landlord had given me. Just in case. Hadn't I seen, in one of the harbours that the boy's questions recalled, how the bosun held a key in his clenched fist so that the tip projected from between his fingers, the steel key tip, then let fly at an attacker and rammed it into the bridge of his nose?

'Turn round!' I said. But he shook his head. 'How can I?' And he trotted on. Again his lower lip thrust out, he was off in a huff, as the bosun would have said. 'And you?' he said, 'Why aren't *you* asking anything? Why don't you ask how *I've* been? You don't know anything. You never heard anything. I just slouched about the houses while you were off travelling the world, walking tall, head held high. No cards, no calls! All these years! Not a word, not of praise, of encouragement, nor a word of advice! Is that how a man treats his son? Even Mother says, it's a crying shame. While I dip my hands in the gutter, you have a fresh wind in your face. While I was making do with pictures, you had women.'

This aimless jabbering continued and I put up with it since I saw that there was no point trying to convince him of his mistake, all the while we walked down from the mine track and into the village. But why call it even a village? A few low houses grouped round a circular green. I looked at my note—the house with the broad eaves—and went into the overgrown garden, with him at my heels, but when he tried to follow me into the house I slammed the door. I heaved my suitcase up onto the bed, went through the rooms—nothing special, small and cold as I had expected—and when I glanced out of the window I saw that he had taken up position next to a fallen tree and was looking up at me. And when he was still standing there at noon, I took a couple of big pieces of firewood from by the stove, went outside and flung them at him.

nine

IT'S NOT FRIDAY YET

I can see the light sweeping over the water again. Is it the watchmen walking along the road, on its raised embankment, watching the water level rise? But what can they do except wait, and if it happens, if the water laps over the road surface, is there anything at all they can do about it except make their report to the crisis management team, sitting back at headquarters in the dry? 'Banks burst.' Then the next morning the helicopters will take off and overfly the region, the fluttering roar up in the sky. And when we look upwards, we'll find ourselves looking into the eye of a camera staring down at us. The cameraman leans over and looks through his viewfinder. Down below, the treetops showing where the road runs, over there the mounds of potash salt thrusting out of the water like breasts, there the huddled trees with roofs peeping between. And that evening we'll watch the images on television, an area the size of the Saarland and hear a voice-over—that is, if we still have a television, if it's not us clinging to the ridge of a roof. But it's still night and all there is to hear right now is the rain splashing down and underneath that, the wind whistling over the old mine track, sometimes higher, sometimes lower. And when a flicker of something like sheet lightning shudders through the clouds,

I see myself at the edge of Vienna on that day in March, between the cold storage and the warehouses in the harbour at Albern, walking round corners in the teeth of a storm, going through alleyways and yards where hardly anyone went back then—the docks had just been rebuilt—and eventually stopping under the canopy of a loading ramp.

Two days ago, after weeks of rain, a lock had burst its gates at a power station upstream, the dammed-up water had rushed out into the Danube floodplains, the catch basins spilt over, the water was swelling at the dykes and downriver, in the Marchland, had flooded some lower-lying villages. All shipping traffic had been stopped, we were tied up in harbour with a load of machine parts bound for Hungary and no one knew when we would get moving again. I had haggled with the harbourmaster about the docking fees and he had said that it could be days, even weeks, before the navigable channels were dredged and declared clear. That morning the rain had stopped and just as we thought we'd seen the worst, the storm began, rain rattling down as though to make up for the missed hours.

It was afternoon and pitch dark except when lightning flashed. The only light that I could see came from the window of a low shed that formed part of a row of workshops. A lamp lit up a table, on which stood a wooden figure, long arms and feeble-looking legs, perhaps it was supposed to be an angel, that is if the shapes on the figure's back were wings and not outsized shoulder blades. It had a sort of helmet or, maybe, cap on its head and its robe (with the legs showing underneath) was covered with spots, as though a swarm of white butterflies had settled there. Now and again two hands showed at the window and turned the figure ever so slightly, but from where I stood I could not see whose hands they were. The shed was diagonally across from me and whoever it was there was hidden by the wall, only his hands showed behind it.

I fumbled for my cigarettes but I had left them in the harbourmaster's office. All I found was my lighter and an address that he had scribbled for me on a sheet of notepaper, the address of a pub where—he said—the food was good value, not far from the quay where we had tied up. I had arrived ten days ago and gone straight on board ship, berthed upriver by the pumping station.

The canopy ran the whole length of the ramp. Luckily it was wide enough, that's to say, as long as the downpour fell straight down it was but as soon as the wind picked up, rain shot in under my shelter so that I had to press my back against the corrugated iron wall and when I looked up, I saw someone in the shed door on the other side of the street. The door had opened, someone had gone to the door and was looking across, or so at least I thought, even though all I saw was an outline, his face was in shadow.

'Hallo,' I called out and waved but there was no answer. He had not seen me. No wonder, I was standing right at the back underneath the roof after all, he was in an open doorway, in front of the light from inside the shed. And my shout had been swallowed up by the roaring rain and grumbling thunder. Now I saw a movement, and when a cigarette lighter sparked up, I saw a woman, it was a woman over there on the other side of the street, the storm, the sheets of rain. She was smoking. Automatically I put my hand in my pocket. But, of course, I had left the cigarettes in the harbourmaster's office. The wind drove the rain straight at me, while she was sheltered by the building where she stood. The smoke didn't rise but settled as clouds round her head and after she had puffed once or twice on the cigarette, making it glow, I heard her words from through the smoke, 'You've come too early. Why today? Go away. It's not Friday yet.'

A young woman, or not yet old. Here in the darkness of the mine track her words strike me with the same clear force they had back then, cutting through the storm and wind in the street. Go away. And add one more fault to my list of omissions? Leaving the house at night, indeed, and walking along the mine track on its embankment because all the asphalt paths are under water—everything that I have failed to do leaps out at me from the dark, my failures lurk in the driving rain, in the whistling sound overhead. You've come too early. Why today. But the rain swept under the roof and slapped at my legs, my shoes and trousers were soaked, it was cold too. Obviously she'd mistaken me for someone else but I could clear that up once I was inside, in the warm, in the dry. On top of which I was craving a smoke. 'All right,' I shouted back. But I was here now and surely, I called out, she'd let me in under the circumstances? She flicked away the cigarette and went back into the workshop but didn't shut the door completely behind her. A crack of light showed, and when the rain let up I leapt out of the ramp and ran across the street.

Dry, yes it was dry, if by that we mean that it was drier than outside, but if I had thought that I was coming into the warmth, then that was a mistake. The only source of heat was an old-fashioned electric heater in a reflector dish, its coil glowing red. And the workshop? If it was a workshop, then it hadn't been built for its current use. Grooves as thick as my arm ran along the concrete floor, leading to deeper run-off channels, and chains hung from iron rails on the ceiling, each doubled over with its hook made fast in an upper link to give headroom for people to pass beneath—the grooves, the chains, the hooks and straightaway I thought that beef and pork carcasses must have hung here, halved. If it was a workshop then the craft practised here was the slaughterman's, but on the other hand, if a slaughterhouse—if slaughterhouse was what it was—then the walls had to be different. They'd be tiled, while these weren't. They were of stone, stone walls with mortar squeezed out between the blocks, scabs of sand here and there along the walls.

'Pardon me,' I called out and looked round, 'If you don't mind, I've just come to take shelter.' And I pointed to my trousers that clung to my legs like bandages from the knees downwards, but there was no one there who might have looked. The woman was nowhere to be seen. A large room, the only light from the lamp at the window, the other side of the room was in darkness, and there in the darkness was a door that led to a yard, to a hallway or to one of the other workspaces. I had come in through one door and she went out the other. Also over in the dark, in the dark half of the room, a mattress with a sleeping bag on it, such as I had taken along hitch-hiking when I was young. In this half of the room there was a sort of camp, the sleeping bag on the mattress and around the mattress a suitcase, a towel, a pullover, a shrivelled apple, a corkscrew, a bottle of mineral water, a candle burnt down to a stub.

I recall all of this now in the pitch black of the mine track, just as I recall the cigarette packet, blue, shining seductively. There were three tables on the window side of the room, one with the angel, covered not with a swarm of butterflies but by slips of white paper pasted like sticking plasters, the second table with the blue packet and a microscope with two eyepieces, the third table with various tools, and as I went closer I recognized only a gouge, brace and bit, screwdriver and clamp, tools that had hung in my grandfather's workshop as well but there were others that I had never seen before, all of them tiny, as though from a toy box (though there was nothing toy-like about them), and scattered among them numberless jars and bottles, brushes, tweezers, plugs of cotton wool and rags. And as I reached for the packet, I heard again, 'It's not Friday yet.' A hollow voice—so hollow that it might have been coming through a chimney pipe. 'No,' I called to the door, 'Friday is tomorrow.' I took the cigarette, shut my hand round it so that it would not get wet and left, and when I was standing once more under the canopy of the ramp, I heard a sound from the doorway, a metallic scratching and scraping, as though a key had been turned or a bolt shot home.

It was still raining but the storm had moved on, and when I lit the cigarette I saw a movement at the window, the woman moved the table with the angel aside, vanished and when she reappeared she had a board in her hand which she leant against the windowpanes, then another board, and when there were three or four, she got up on a chair and began to nail them over the opening, and while she did this it had grown somewhat lighter, it could almost have been called daylight. A grey-blue patch appeared westwards in the overcast and the ceaselessly shifting clouds scudded over the sky and I could make out a few details of the street, which had been nothing but a dark chasm before—the gutter running the whole length of the sheds had burst, the water had run off the roof, down the walls and into the masonry, so that patches were visible in the upper part of the wall, once yellow. Letters had fallen from the company name over the door, leaving only EL . . . OTR . . . A. The pouring, splashing rain gave way to drips and drops, the canopy over the ramp dripped too and a thick, clay-brown torrent ran down the carelessly paved street.

Daylight returned but the woman was doing all she could to block it out. Had she not noticed the change? The sound of hammering rang out between the drips and drops all round, so that I threw away the cigarette, walked up to the window and pointed to the sky. She had already fastened the first board and now she picked up the second. I stepped through the clay-brown torrent that ran over the pavement, stood in front of the window, lifted my hand—Look there, the rain has stopped, it's clearing up!—but she looked past me. It was hard to make out her face behind the pane, her hair seemed to be blonde and was held back by a band that also covered her ears, a dark smock with a small, gleaming knife showing in a pocket, and she was holding two nails between her lips. She stood on the chair, balanced the board and when she placed it across the window I turned round and walked down the kerbstone, which stood clear of the water. I walked along the street, back to the ship. Exactly as described in my letter, for the attention of the Vienna-West Police Authority. In the yards further down the hill the water was knee-deep, little whirlpools had formed here and there, where the rubbish swept along by the rain swirled in ever tighter spirals—scraps of paper, the unidentifiable remains of objects that may have been useful once—and there was a gurgling, champing sound in the air, as though many mouths were chewing, swallowing the detritus down into the earth where it would be digested.

Clearly, I had been walking in a zigzag before, now I simply followed the street and came to the building where I had sat with the harbourmaster. The little office—really a sub-office, overseeing this small stretch of docks—was huddled between the warehouses, all locked up because of the floods, their doors fastened with chains. On one of the doors someone had written in white chalk, the words now smeared, *Wherever you look, use your own eyes*. I stood in front of the harbourmaster's office and wanted to smoke again. I went up the stairs but my cigarettes lay behind a locked door, clocking-off time, they had all gone home. Or had the harbourmaster taken his team to a crisis conference in the Westhafen, to meet the main-port authority? Hadn't he said that every drop that fell could unleash catastrophe? Down here by the quayside, sandbags were stacked up to form barriers, waist-high.

It wasn't a good ship, that one, the crew were awkward. Mirko, the bosun, kept falling asleep, and Herbert, the mechanic, liked the sound of his own voice, and all night long music pounded from his cabin (or something he called music). His cabin was next to mine, when I thumped on the wall he would turn the radio down, which almost made it worse since all I could hear then was the thudding of the bass.

Mirko was a short, taciturn man in his mid-fifties, with ash-grey hair that stood up from his head like bristles from a brush. His working papers said that he was a Yugoslav, but as I came on board, Herbert had taken me aside and whispered, glancing at Mirko, 'Skipper, he's a Croat.' I can still remember—we were standing on deck, Mirko sat a little further off on one of the hatches, he had tilted his head back and shut his eyes, although there was no knowing whether he had his eyes shut because he was asleep or because of the sun, no knowing indeed whether his eyes were really shut or whether he wasn't peering at us through hooded lids and when Herbert realized this he turned round and walked further off. Sometime people came aboard, little old men who would take Mirko in their arms. They would go down to his cabin and when I went past I noticed that the curtains were shut, though a moment ago they had been open, not a word could be heard, not a sound, so I wondered what they were doing in there. There wasn't much elbow room on that ship, that's to say it was narrow-built but the crew were prickly people as well. It wasn't my ship, I was simply a replacement, relief captain. I'd come in to take over from the actual captain, who had fallen ill, and I wanted to get the journey over and done with. In early March on the day when I took the command, the sun was shining but then the thaws came, the snowmelt, the rain, and we were laid up for weeks on end.

The crates with the machine parts were stowed in the hold but since they didn't all fit there, the rest were stacked up on the hatches, covered with tarpaulin and lashed down with cable—a few days ago another boat in this same part of the harbour had had its whole cargo stolen. While the crew were sitting in a bar, a lot of lorries had rolled up, one of the men had shown the crane operator some papers that seemed to say that delivery was cancelled for that cargo. And when the crew came back, they stood in front of an empty hold.

Mirko was sitting at the bridge, as I had told him to time and again—from there you could see the quay, the deck and the crates, but his arms were folded, his head sunk so that all I could see from a distance was his bristly hair. When I came in, he woke with a start. He was asleep, had been sleeping. But what could I say? That he should keep his eyes open, if it wasn't too much trouble? That there were others keeping their eyes open, prying eyes at that, and any lapse of attention on our part . . . oh, he knew all that, knew it all, so all I said was, 'Get below! Go lie down! I'll stay above.' But first I went down to my cabin, changed trousers and pocketed some cigarettes, and when I came above again he was back where he had been, arms folded, head down, eyes closed. He did his work, no question, but as soon as he sat down or even leant against anything, his head would drop.

About ten o'clock I saw Herbert at the end of the quay, it was dark but the lamps had been switched on, he walked under the loading bridge in his German army jacket, then came aboard a moment later, his footsteps echoing, and as soon as he opened the door he started chatting away. No, not a good ship, not a good crew, one always falling asleep, the other trotting about the place in an army jacket, talking nineteen to the dozen and leaving his radio on all night. And myself? I dithered, I snapped at them and spoke sharply, then took back what I had said with the next breath.

So, just after ten I gave Herbert the watch, went to my cabin, lay down, then got up again a couple of minutes later and went across to Mirko. He was lying on his back in his bunk, arms under his head, his eyes open. 'Mirko,' I said, 'do you have any cigarettes?' I had taken my last packet up to the bridge earlier. He sat up and pointed at a pouch of tobacco, true enough, he smoked Russian tobacco, *makhorka*, rolled his own, I shook my head, no thanks, and went up to the bridge, but before I had even got there I remembered that Herbert didn't smoke, so I turned about, fetched my jacket and went down the gangway once more.

If I'm trying to remember every detail, every word and every step, then it's also because I want to be sure in my mind that I had already forgotten the woman—I had other concerns, the ship, the cargo, the crew, how I could get everything down the river in one piece—and that it was a coincidence that I saw her again. If Mirko had smoked anything else but Russian or if Herbert had cigarettes, I would have stayed on board.

The pub that the harbourmaster had told me about had to be somewhere near, in one of the alleys leading down to this square. It was still raining, or raining again, but this was a harmless sort, you knew that rain like this would stop soon enough, while the one earlier had looked set to go on like that forever—weeks, months, years. The water was inches deep on the quayside and level with the water in the harbour itself (impossible to see where the one began and the other ended), reaching right across to the flickering lights on the other side of the harbour. Since I had solid ground beneath my feet, for a moment I thought it must be possible to walk right out past the boats, across the water.

She was sitting with her back to the door in one of the booths along the walls, narrow neck, that hairband, the blonde hair, and now, as I recall other details in the darkness of the mine track, I think that she was wearing the pullover that had been lying on the mattress that afternoon. I went up to the bar and asked for a carton of cigarettes. The landlord, a tall, heavyset man wearing a leather apron, turned round, opened a cupboard, took one out and put it on the bar, and once I had paid I went across to her table. She had her head down, turning an empty glass in her gloved hands, the gloves cut off at the knuckles like cyclist's gloves but they weren't leather or some such, they were woollen, and a few loose threads showed that she had cut the fingers off after she bought them.

'Pardon me,' I said, 'for coming into your workshop this afternoon the way that . . . but the storm, you know, the rain.'

She looked up, meaning that she looked at the zip on my jacket, which I only done up halfway, then dropped her head again, and since I thought that she had not understood me, I went on, 'This afternoon. I'm sorry if I startled you.' The landlord looked across, one hand on the beer pump, the other on his hip. It occurred to me that since arriving, I had only ever spoken to men. Herbert, Mirko, the harbourmaster, a few other skippers who had tied up at the same quay, all of them men, leaving aside the barmaid at the pub up by the pumping station—we had gone there a few times, but she wasn't a woman, a girl rather, and even while serving wore headphones which leaked the same sort of irritating rattle that I heard from Herbert's cabin. 'Anyway,' I said, 'I helped myself to a cigarette,' tearing open the carton and taking out a packet. 'Not your brand, I know, but perhaps you'd like to take it anyway.'

She stared at the tabletop the whole time, so that to not admit defeat I was forced to keep talking. 'I'm a boatman, you know, a skipper.' I told her how I came to be standing under the loading ramp, how I saw the light in her workshop, then I told her how we were treading on one another's toes on board, of my crew's shortcomings, then I ended up by talking about other rivers, the Elbe, the Thames, the Hudson, and as though that weren't enough, suddenly I began to talk about my grandfather, about the shed where his tools hung, tools like those in her workshop, and about his garden right by the canal towpath, the smell of the reeds at night and the shimmering willows, and about the burn mark on my back, how it itched under certain conditions. All this burst out in an embarrassing stream of drivel, I heard myself jumping from one story to another as Herbert did when I listened to him, and when I asked her if I could sit down she lifted her head and said in a low but firm voice, 'It's not Friday yet.'

Yes, I can hear her voice now through the wind that whistles over the mine track, and I see her take the raincape that had lain on the seat next to her, a grey cape of some heavy fabric that might have been made from an old tarpaulin or tent.

When I went back to the bar, the landlord narrowed his eyes. I said that I knew her and nodded toward the door. She had simply stood up, put on the cape and left. He looked at me and asked what it would be. 'White wine.' At which he finally took his hand off the pump handle and bent down to open the fridge. Only a few guests left. A Polish skipper I had spoken to about the berthing fees, about how we had to pay full rates (even though this was a clear case of *force majeure*), was feeding coins into a machine at the wall. Two men in blue disaster-relief overalls were watching the television in the corner, which had the sound switched off. It showed water pouring through a little town, then cut away, and showed pictures taken from a helicopter, treetops sticking up from the water, a roof where people sat waving their arms, a door spinning about in an eddy and a large wooden bridge collapsing under the onslaught of the flood, then the camera zoomed in on a dog, paddling, holding its muzzle up out of the water, until it was seized by a current and swept out of shot.

I drank a mouthful of wine and as I put the glass down on the bar I noticed a fat woman in a dressing gown in the door to the back room. She must have been asleep, for she held her hand to her mouth and yawned as she watched the images. The dressing gown was white and hung open a little at the front, showing the folds of her mighty bosom. Perhaps she had got up again to see what the news had to say about the flood. Yes, it seemed so, since when I looked again during the world news, she had gone back into the room. Green light came through the half-open door, as though from a shaded bedside lamp. I recall that as well, now, the green light where we were sitting just a little later.

The landlord was going from table to table and whispering to the guests and the men from disaster relief pulled out their wallets in response and gave him two banknotes, one each. A man sitting on his own in one of the booths, a dock-hand, judging by the way he was dressed, lifted his hand from the table, and now I saw the note that had been hidden under it, a hundred schillings, which the landlord whipped into his apron as he went past. The Pole had turned his back on the slot machine and walked toward him waving a note, the landlord plucked it from his hand, then looked at me. 'Now then, skipper, what's it to be? I'm locking up now. If you want to stay, you'll have to pay, unless of course,' he winked, 'you want to take Ricky's place.'

When the name Ricky was mentioned, a boy got up from the corner where he had been sleeping, head on hands and stumbled across to the door where the woman in the dressing gown had stood. I thought of the narrow ship, the bunk, the rhythmical thudding from Herbert's cabin, I didn't want to go back there, and I took out a note, a hundred schillings, the same amount I had seen in the Pole's hand and on the table where the dockhand sat. The landlord pocketed the note and went to the front door, where he turned the key. The others had got up and gone to the door, where the light shone green. Ricky rubbed the sleep from his eyes, pulling a sour face as though he had been ordered to climb into the anchor locker to free a jammed chain. He wore a yellow jacket of imitation leather (rather like Mirko's), light jeans and cowboy boots with pearls down the calves, and didn't take these off the whole time. His hair hung down his brow and he had a small scar under the left eye. After we had gone through the door, the landlord leading, he slumped into a chair, stuck his legs out and folded his arms. The men from disaster relief sat down together, while the Pole, the dockhand and I made sure that we each had at least one free chair between us.

The green light came from two lamps up under the ceiling, pointed down at a podium in the middle of the room, the two rows of chairs were arranged in semicircles in front, and dimly in the background were a stool, a washbasin and the couch where the woman in the dressing gown was stretched out. She lay on her side, her face turned towards us a full, round face that in this light seemed like a flat disc. As the first bars of 'Strangers in the Night' sounded she sat up with a great deal of effort and put her feet into the slippers that stood in front of the couch, then shook them off again straightaway and stepped instead into a pair of pumps standing next to the washbasin. Then the landlord's voice. I turned round when I heard it. He took two steps forward, spread his arms and called out like a ringmaster, 'Frau Mona!'

Now she squeezed through a gap between the chairs, climbed up onto the platform, turned round twice and let the dressing gown slip from her shoulders, but caught it at the last moment, feigning shock and tugging it closed over her bosom, then pouted her lips to sketch blowing a kiss. The light had changed, the green had been switched off and red came on so that her shoulders shone like legs of lamb, glistening pink, she danced forward and back a few steps, then let her dressing gown fall, and as she turned round and round, surprisingly nimble, showing herself to us from all sides, the landlord came forward, stepped up on the platform and said, 'Gentlemen, it's your turn now. Frau Mona waits. Whoever can mount her without being thrown off will get his money back.' He held up a hundred schilling note. 'Come along, gents, don't be so shy, she won't bite.'

An embarrassed laugh from the emergency relief workers in the front row, who put their heads together. The Pole looked at the floor, the dockhand rummaged in his pockets as though looking for cigarettes, I looked about the place as though it was all nothing to do with me, looked at the couch, the washbasin, up at the spotlights, and Frau Mona danced, turning about her axis on her pumps, which were all she was wearing now, and shaking her arms as though playing the tambourine. The mounds of her flesh (she was fat, but not flabby) began to shake in waves shuddering down from her shoulders, her flesh trembling, rolling and quaking. 'How's that, gentlemen? No one?' The landlord looked about, mimed astonishment and put the banknote back in his pocket. 'Then it's down to Ricky, I suppose.'

Ricky had fallen asleep, or at least I could see his arms and chest rise and fall. Now he stood up, swaying, and took off his jacket, dropped it on the chair and shuffled forward while 'Je t'aime' suddenly moaned from the loudspeakers. He unbuckled his belt as he came forward, tugged his shirt over his head and jumped up onto the platform—a listless sort of jump, he almost fell as he landed but recovered at the last moment—where Mona greeted him with a slap on the backside, then danced on while he strutted about and flexed his muscles, bent his arms and clenched his fists, though he was so skinny—just skin and bone—that we could see every one of his ribs. The Pole was looking forward again, had lifted his eyes a while ago, and the dockhand had given up looking for whatever it was, sat there and looked ahead to where Mona was kneeling down and had put her hands on Ricky's trousers while he still stood, biceps flexed, arms out, grinning at the darkness and the rows of chairs, and only dropped the pose when Mona undid his trousers and peeled them away from his backside, then he grabbed her hair and shoved her head between his legs—she had black curls on her head, though her pubic hair had been shaved off—with his trousers rucked up round his boots and his underwear, a polka-dot posing pouch, hung down above knees bent forward just a little as though to offer himself to Mona, who held her great balloon-like breasts in both hands and was rubbing them on his thighs; we could see as soon as she tugged his trousers down that his cock was half hard, a huge great thing, he pumped his hips so that it flew up and down like a rope-end, slapping her chin, her forehead, her nose, it almost looked as though he were beating her with it; she lunged at it until finally she caught it in her mouth and swallowed, and now we could see her cheeks fill out, her round face seemed to grow even wider; her hands grabbed his balls, she had let go of her breasts and put her hands between his legs; he was straddling so widely that the underwear stretched out between his knees seemed about to tear, the elastic cut into his skin; suddenly, he pushed her away and she rolled onto her back as though this was what she had been waiting for and put her legs in the air, while she spread her labia apart with both hands so that we could see inside, as though this were a butcher's shop, into her, a place that must otherwise have been shut away by rolls of swelling, sagging fat, she proffered it to us while her eyes looked past Ricky into the darkness—yes, I remember that too, in the darkness of the mine track—lying flat on her back, legs up, then suddenly lifted her head and her eyes swept across the audience, serious, quizzical, looking at each one of us in turn for a second, we stared at her and she stared back into the darkness, then she dropped her head, and we heard moaning.

Ricky's penis was stiff now, it was even longer but had lost girth, become thinner, as though some exchange had happened, from girth to length, he showed it to us, that's to say he showed us his erection by turning side-on as though to say, look at that! then got down on his knees and plunged his head between Mona's legs; his underwear sat on top of the jeans now, and his boots poked out from the jeans legs, the heels thrust up in the air while the toes dug into the floor as he began to lick her.

It was a clear night outside, the sky was scattered with stars, the rain had stopped, the wind had died down, the outline of the warehouses showed sharply and the black smell of the canals hung over the alleyways. The two men from disaster relief crossed the street and vanished into an alley between two buildings whose gables met above. The Pole turned up his collar and walked quickly toward the docks—without looking at me or waiting for me—and the dockhand made for a street that led off to one side. The Pole and I would be going the same way but after a moment's hesitation I headed after the dockhand, walking slowly, keeping a distance between us, since I didn't want to talk to him. When the land-lord opened the door for us to leave—'We'd be honoured to see you again soon, gentlemen!'—he had asked what else was still open round here. 'Where next? Where are we going now?' He looked round at us as he spoke. Was I mistaken? If he was a dockhand, then he worked hereabouts and he would have to know the area, he must know it—but his clothing, his posture, his hands—no, he was a dockhand for sure but, of course, he could be off one of the boats. Be that as it may, I didn't want to have to lend an ear now that he had become garrulous.

He swayed a little as he walked, stopped once and leant against the wall, I stopped at the same time so as not to catch up with him. And when he walked on I lit the cigarette that I had been holding in my hand, had not lit before so that he would not notice my light. It was fully dark, the street lamps turned off and even the spotlights that usually burnt day and night to light up company names and signs on the ware-houses had been switched off for some unfathomable reason. And it was quiet. We heard nothing but our own footsteps, his and mine, and I tried little by little to match my pace to his, our footsteps became ever more uniform so that after a while only one set of steps echoed down the street. It was as though we walked under a huge dome, cutting us off from the world, until I came back to my senses with a start at the smell of the canal, no, not a smell like the canal where my grandfather had tied up his boat, a different smell—a rotten, stagnant smell, as though we had taken a wrong turn into the sewer tunnels.

The docker or deckhand kept parallel with the river, then turned aside and stumbled down the street to the square where the harbourmaster's building stood, where I had sat earlier, and as he turned (or rather, as I did) I realized where the smell was coming from, and the sound, that I had imagined was stars knocking against our dome. Water was gushing from the storm drains uphill, running across the paving stones in streams that fanned and spread, the lower part of the square was already flooded, an empty sack hung in one of the chains locked across a silo door, and the writing on the middle door had either been washed away or was already under water. A silent flood, as the newspapers reported later. The real disaster areas were elsewhere, in the plains and the villages downriver, where thousands of volunteers had gathered and had pitched their own tent cities, while hereabouts there were only a few sandbags, brought in haphazardly and stacked up. A flood that might have passed totally unnoticed if the damage had not been discovered the next day, the filth, the slime, the dissolving shit that had floated up to the surface, thanks to an error in the control system where the pipes were all connected, once the barrages had burst—or perhaps someone had pressed the wrong button or turned the wrong lever (and it was hushed up later), opening the locks and diverting the river into the canals, maybe it was human error, but whatever it was, the end result was that I couldn't get back—tonight there was no way to get down to the river, the docks, the boats.

We had come out onto the upper part of the square, the part next to the harbourmaster's office that was still dry, and were looking at the gushing storm drains and the dark soupy flow that lapped and rose, that's to say, I was looking, the docker or deckhand had sat down on the harbourmaster's front steps and was looking at me. 'Come here, brother of mine! Where can we get a drink?' Then he shuffled to one side to show me that I should sit down. One hand was in his pocket, he held the other in front of his face. 'Give me a cigarette!' But I went on past the harbourmaster's office and turned into a street that led uphill, a street covered with a thin sheet of mud. And once again, I heard the knocking sound—I knew now that it came from the canals—the canals knocking as they spewed their guts out onto the square, and as I went further from the square the sound died away and I heard footsteps. The docker or deckhand? Was he coming after me? I turned round, no, the street was empty, a sickle moon had risen, the stars were white pinpricks, warehouses towered left and right, then soon gave way to smaller buildings, a row of sheds built up against one another, up ahead of me the loading ramps stretched out over the street offering shelter, on my right, while on my left thin chinks of light glinted from the cracks between the boards.

The lamps were lit, the electricity was back. Or had it not even been cut out up here, roughly the same altitude as the pub? And when I put my eye to the window, I saw two hands turning the angel, as that afternoon, and only then did I see the woman, sitting on a stool and looking thoughtfully at the angel and at the strips of paper stuck all over it. Then she leant back, put her hands together in her lap and her lips moved as though she were talking to it, then she stood up, peeled off one of the strips, took the speck of wood or paint clinging to it and placed it on a glass slide. She put in under the microscope and looked through the eyepieces.

I know now that these specks of wood or paint are called *Schollen*, clods. Months later a restorer explained the process to me and said that sometimes these clods simply didn't stick. A restorer would take the loose fragment from the wood, clean it, daub it with glue, replace it and put a strip of paper across to hold it down, but when you remove the paper, the fragments just fall out again onto your bench. Why? Perhaps the item had been exposed to strong heat in the past, or sometimes the old masters had applied a layer of silver to the wood, bedding it down with chalk, to make the colours shine. The chalk was the problem, since it wouldn't bond with the glue. Centuries of heat, damp, dry or cold had made it unpredictable, altered the consistency. Often enough, you could spend months looking for a solution and not come a step nearer, some problems were simply insoluble. I know this now but at the time I only saw her back. She leant over, straightened up and when she turned round I lifted my hand and knocked on the pane. 'Pardon me!' She was still awake, she was standing inside, I stood outside. It was cold out there, perhaps I could go in, perhaps we could talk.

She dropped the glass slide as soon as she heard my knock and took a step to the side at the same time so that I was left looking straight into the lamplight, and just as I decided that she had crossed to the other side of the room, the dark half, I heard her voice. The woman had stepped against the wall by the window and said, 'It's not Friday yet.' It was two o'clock in the morning. 'You're wrong,' I replied. 'Today's Friday.' And yet I knew that there was no point arguing with her. Even if I could speak with the tongues of angels (which I can't), she would refuse to unlock the door. And when I suggested that I stay outside and speak to her through the window, the light was turned off inside and I heard, 'Leave now.'

Then I turned and walked on, up the street, and for a while I could still hear that singsong voice from the distance, a voice that soon sounded to me like bubbling water—Friday, Friday—an endlessly repeating sound, and when I came to a crossroads on the street, I saw the docker or deckhand. He was leaning down to the window of a car stopped in an entranceway, a large limousine with tinted glass, the window rolled up silently, the docker or deckhand turned round and I said, 'How did you get up here?' He looked at me without answering, a man of middle height, late forties, a hard face, work-worn hands that hung from the sleeves of his jacket, a grey cap that fit snugly to his head, a cap that he had not taken off even in the pub.

Which is why, *officers*—yes, now I remember the phrasing of the letter I wrote weeks later in Pressburg—*since I have only now learnt of the crime from a newspaper report, I feel I must tell you what I saw that night*. Anyway, the docker or deckhand had snapped out of his drunken chatty mood and was squaring up in a threatening manner. What I didn't write down but what I remembered later is that in the ten minutes between our meeting at the harbourmaster's office and then at the crossroads, he had changed completely. He stood there motionless and watched me with his eyes narrowed, as though he didn't quite know what to do with me or as though waiting for a signal from inside the car where I couldn't see. I can't say what the passengers looked like or how many they were. The moonlight gleamed off the black paintwork. Once, I thought I saw a cigarette end glowing, a red dot that lit up behind the window and then died away.

That was on 19 March, Friday, about half past two. I know the exact date because I made a note in the ship's log that the lower harbour had been flooded. By about midday the muddy water had withdrawn far enough for me to go on board without wading through it, the slime clung to the walls a metre high in the warehouse district and a stench hung in the air . . . it was so repellent that Herbert stayed down in the engine room and declared that he had repairs to make, just so that I couldn't put him to work on deck, while Mirko had a Russian cigarette burning between his lips the whole time, held just so, with the smoke rising into his nostrils to over-power all other smells, I breathed in shallow gulps, and when I looked out of the window in the evening I saw that the Pole had a cloth tied round his face as he marched under the loading bridge toward the harbourmaster's office or the pub.

That was on Friday and on the next day, Saturday, I left. The ship owners were expecting my report. The three boats on the company books were registered in Austria but they traded from a small office in a little town on the lower Rhine. I was on a train the whole night. I had left Mirko in charge of the boat and he called every evening to keep me up to date (or rather, the company, since I never spoke to him myself) and at the beginning of April, when we heard that we could finally expect shipping to resume, I was ordered back to Vienna.

Yes, by early April the waters had dropped far enough for us to get underway finally, there was still water in the meadows but the navigable channel was clear, marked with barrels floating on the water one after the other. We sailed at half power, for any wash we made would have worsened the damage already done to the banks, but the current was strong enough to push us along downstream at quite a rate—the water was an unhealthy, mud-brown colour, and flocks of cormorants sat on treetops rearing out of the water. I watched them through the telescope, big black birds that took flight with short, powerful beats of their wings, then suddenly shot back down into the water.

Mirko sat behind me on the bridge and when we tied up in Pressburg, he leapt ashore, not using the gangplank, then I saw him turn into an alley between buildings, and when I asked Herbert what this was supposed to be about, he shrugged his shoulders and only said, 'Skipper, he's a Croat.' He stood on the quayside by the bollard where he had tied up. It was late afternoon, the sun shining just above the rooftops, two girls sitting in front of a warehouse with their legs up on a chair and their skirts pushed up. Herbert looked across at them, opened his mouth as though to say something, then waved his hand dismissively, stomped up the gangplank and opened the engine-room door. I went to my cabin, opened the log and wrote, 7 April, Pressburg, Pozsony, Bratislava—the same dateline as the letter I wrote that evening but didn't send—yes, now I see myself sitting in the cabin and staring at the photograph in the newspaper.

Mirko came back about half past seven. It was still light but dusk had already set in, his jacket glowed brightly in front of the rusty black buildings on the street across from the quays. He wore the same yellow imitation leather jacket with its countless pockets and as he came onto the bridge he burrowed about in these and produced various objects, unbuttoning the pockets, taking out the items and putting them one next to the other on the map table—a roll of brown tape, nail scissors, a handful of crooked nails, a corkscrew, a pair of tongs gleaming silver. I said, 'Mirko, what is all this? Where've you been? Why did you leave?'

He bent over the table, I saw his back, the back of his head, his brush of hair, then he turned round and went on deck, to the first hatch, where he leant against a crate. And now, at the end of the row of objects he had put down on the table, I saw the newspaper, it was the *Kurier*. Mirko had folded the pages back so that I could not miss the photograph. I turned on the light above the map table, shone it on the picture and then went out to ask him, Mirko, where did you get that newspaper? But he wasn't there.

The newspaper was dated 23 March, the Tuesday. I wanted to ask him whether he'd found it by chance. He wasn't in his cabin either. In the photograph her eyes were half closed, she was looking at the viewer with half-closed eyes and seemed to be wearing the same smock and the same hairband, but a second glance showed that her forehead and throat were covered, it was a cloth lying over her forehead and her neck . . . and some kind of veil over her face, as though this was a reconstruction or the photograph had been retouched to spare the viewer some of the details. The article called her *the unknown woman*—an unknown woman, between thirty-five and forty years old, had been found dead in the premises of the Wotruba rope factory, abandoned since the sixties. The chains hanging from the ceiling weren't mentioned, nor were the mattress and its little camp, the tables, the tools, the lamp, the heating arrangements, the angel, but instead it reported that the floor was clean, as though it had been swept and then hosed down, and that crumpled strips of paper, all the same length, had been found in a drain by the door. Death had occurred some time early on Friday morning.

'Herbert, have you seen Mirko?'

He shook his head, he was sitting on the bollard and staring over at the building where the girls had been sitting. So I locked up the bridge, went to my cabin and cleared the desk.

Wednesday, 7 April. Dear Sir/Madam, I have just learnt that. Then I crossed out the sentence and began again . . . *since I have just . . . I would like to inform you that.* The desk was by the window, it had grown dark by now, the lamp threw a white circle of light on the paper. Once (about ten, I looked at the clock) a helicopter came down low over the river, its searchlights on, so close that I saw the water splash in the downdraught of the rotors—that flapping, roaring sound in the air—and only climbed at the very last moment, when it seemed that it would smash into the rooftops, then it was quiet again, so quiet that I could hear the ship settle and crack, hear the ship breathe, stretch itself, draw up snug again, and the water lapping against the hull. I wrote slowly—the storm, the flood, the docker, the crossroads, the car. Then I leant back and folded my hands behind my head and at that moment I saw a red dot light up behind the window—

the cigarette glowed, dimmed, and Mirko said, 'Tomorrow is Friday.'

The window was open just a crack. I wanted to answer, You're wrong, but it was true, he was right, midnight had passed, Thursday had begun. 'Skipper, I don't want to make any threats but we saw you near the workshop that night and we don't rightly know what we should make of it.' I went out to talk to him but he wasn't there, he was standing on the quay. Two lorries drew up, a man came aboard, shoved past me, scuttled to the first hatch and set about snipping the steel cable over the wooden crates with a set of long-handled bolt cutters. Then I turned round, went back into my cabin, wrote down the address on the envelope—any information pertinent to the enquiry should be addressed to—put the letter inside, sealed it and tore it into tiny pieces.

ten

THE KEY

The bus slid out of the clouds covering the mountains, not even high mountains at that, crept down the hairpin bends and vanished behind the trees, coming back into sight a little later on the stretch of road below. I squatted on the sloping mountainside and dug my heels into the grass to keep myself from slipping, and now I could see that it was a blue bus, one of the blue-liveried public buses that ran between the villages in the region where I ended up (though this was not that region, for there it was flat). It vanished again and came back from the other direction, and when it drew level with me I recognized it. It was the bus we had climbed into by the electricity substation. It passed so close that I could see the driver's face, his hands hanging on the steering wheel like damp rags, the villagers in the rows of seats behind him, including Werner and Maren, I saw all of us being driven along the steep road—and heard my grandfather's voice at the same time, 'For he can travel through Germany, through Poland, through Russia as far as Asia through the lands of the Mohammedans and the heathens, crossing from land to water, from water back to land, on and on.' He was reading from the book he had picked out as my guide to the world

148

and its ways, but when I turned round, I saw not him, but a bush, with the words flickering out from it—

When I opened my eyes, I must have nodded off, it was dark, dark outside and dark in the bus, the lights above our seats had been switched off and only the colourful smaller lights of the driver's dashboard glowed, visible all the way down the central aisle, and, of course, the headlights were visible too, casting light a little way ahead of us up the road. The rain drove at us in irregular gusts, sometimes it seemed even to stop and then the rumbling of the motor could be heard for a moment, the tyres singing on the road surface, then it would teem down again, rattling down as though someone were throwing gravel onto the roof, and the windscreen wipers would sweep the water aside once more, having spent a little while beating at nothing.

My watch showed ten o'clock, ten in the evening, not late by any means, but people were slumped asleep in their seats, they'd been waiting for this bus since morning, waited for a bus that did not come, that only appeared late in the afternoon, then wound its way endlessly from one village to the next before turning onto the motorway. They had grumbled and let the driver know what they thought of him but that murmur had died down now and instead there were only occasional sighs as though their dreams troubled them, and the driver himself uttered a few sounds which might have been curses, though I preferred the silence in which he had wrapped himself earlier. Headquarters had sent him to fetch us to safety, a man neither tall nor short. In a situation like ours, we wanted explanations, a friendly face, encouragement but we soon enough realized that this man couldn't satisfy these needs—either because he was exhausted or he didn't know or he was not the type. He had a smeared, vague face with watery eyes, and looking at him you had no idea whether those eyes even saw you clearly or only saw as through a haze (or a film of water). The simplest of questions—what's our route? our destination? time of arrival?—glanced off him, or rather, they sank into him like a stone flung into a sump, without leaving a ripple. Perhaps his swearing meant that he had awoken from his daze and was wondering why he had not dropped us off long ago, in one of the emergency shelters that were supposedly being set up at the edge of the floods.

I stood up and went to the front to ask him. Surely he must know how far we still had to go. But he pointed forward, as though to say, You can see for yourself. Though all I saw was that the situation was quite different now. Rain? Yes. But only showers, the pauses between them longer, while earlier it had been an unbroken downpour. As for driving conditions—when we set off we could hardly turn into a road without coming to a stop a few kilometres further on, faced with impassable water, then he would turn round, drive back, and when we thought we could get under way again, a clear run, the road would slope imperceptibly and lead down to another dell where we saw the roofs of a village poking out of the water, surrounded by floating rubbish. But now we were rolling along, dead ahead, and there was no more cause to claim that the weather or the route were slowing our arrival. Now and then cars passed us the other way, and if I wasn't mistaken once we could even see the lights of a town.

'How far is it? When are we arriving?'

But he pressed his lips together, inasmuch as I can even say that this man made any clear movements, that his mouth showed his thoughts. It was more that his lips met and then parted again, smacking. And when I went back, I saw Maren. Her head was drooping on her shoulder, her eyes shut, her legs turned to the side, her hands between them, so that I could imagine how the backs of her hands touched the inside of her thighs.

Werner sat on the other side of the aisle. His hand hung down and I didn't for a moment doubt that before he fell asleep he had reached out toward her. 'Maren,' he would have said, 'Maren, are you all right?' Just as he had said on the day I arrived, when we stood by the fence and he beckoned her over. 'Maren, our new neighbour!' She came, gave me her hand, that's to say her hand went past mine, a long, bony hand that passed mine by and briefly grabbed my wrist, then she turned and went to the stables on the other side of the farmyard; still young, perhaps in her late thirties, rather short, thin, hair straggling over half her face. Jeans, grey pullover, boots on her feet (not the gumboots I saw later but leather boots), town boots with their zippers pulled all the way down to the ankles so that the calves flopped over and dragged on the paving. Her husband watched her go. He was heavily built, his face weather-beaten but for two clear patches under his eyes that gleamed like mirrors—when he turned his head I thought I saw my reflection disappear. 'Maren,' he called, 'Maren, are you all right?' On the afternoon of that same day there was a knock on my door and when I opened it, she came in, and the next day too.

That had been early October. Rain? Yes. But only drizzle and we still thought that it would stop some time, while in fact it was just the beginning, the beginning of a rainy stretch which would end (if it had ended at all) with us climbing aboard the bus.

'Werner,' I said as I came past them, 'Werner.' But he was asleep, his mouth open, his hand hung down while her hands were clamped between her legs.

I had looked at their house three days ago. It was around two, two o'clock at night and I was coming back from the mine track, the only road not under water yet, and just as I was opening the garden gate, I heard a noise, a clattering, turned about and saw that it came from next door. A shutter had slipped its catch and was banging the wall of the house, then swung back and a new gust of wind came and the shutter slammed against the wall once more. After a while the window opened, a hand reached out, pulled the shutter to, the bar shot home, the window closed and all was quiet again, except for the hiss of the rain sweeping across the village green, a sound that had become as natural as a heartbeat, hardly noticeable. And as I stood there I felt something swelling inside me, involuntarily I crossed my arms on my chest to stop whatever it was from bursting me into tiny pieces. For weeks now, I had felt it tugging me, tearing me. One voice said, Go! and another said, Stay!, and I had only ever felt this way at leavetakings, at partings—it was desire and its opposite, swelling and shrinking, a feeling that tore me apart one moment and crushed me to a pulp the next. But time swelled and shrank as well, and there was a little of the same nerve-wracking need in the way I waited there for the shutter's next slam. I looked up at the window and then walked across the round village green, long flooded by now, and when I went through the garden gate I saw the water.

Only an hour ago it had been puddled in the garden's dips and depths, now it covered great stretches of the paved path that led to the house.

The next day was 16 December (you will be able to look up the date in every account of the floods that they publish). When the muddy water seeped through under my door I swung down my suitcase, packed days ago, and hauled it up the ladder into the space between the beams and the rooftop, a loft of sorts that hardly came up to my waist. The man I rented from was a city dweller who thought it was a fine thing to own a house in the country, though he didn't live in it, and this was where he had stowed away all the lumber bought from the farmers round about in an initial surge of enthusiasm—a spinning wheel, a rusty scythe, earthenware jugs. There was a window, or a hatch, at floor level up in the attic, and I lay there watching the water rise—by noon it was at the sharp tips of the fence posts, by evening it had reached the lower branches of the nut tree, and when I shone my torch out at midnight, only the crown of the tree could be seen. The water rose as though the earth were a giant sponge and someone were squeezing it now, releasing all the rain it had soaked up in recent months.

There was a power cut around noon. The telephone was in one of the rooms downstairs, and last time I looked down through the hatch the muddy water was practically up to the ceiling. In the afternoon, noises floated across from the village, the grumble of motors, a metallic rattling, the dull thump of wood on wood, voices, 'Hey, hey,' stamping hooves, slamming doors, and I heard it all as though through damp cotton wool stuffed into my ears, then there was quiet and all I could hear was the racket of the rain sweeping through the garden and hammering on the roof above my head. Now it serves me right, I thought, lying there in a crowded lumber room, looking out through the window as darkness fell, now it serves me right that I never spoke more than two or three words to anyone in the village—apart from Werner and Maren. If I went out at all, it was at night, so perhaps the villagers believed that I had left as suddenly as I had turned up in the first place and they didn't even stop to wonder, Where is that man we sometimes saw?

That morning though there was a tap at the windowpane and when I looked out, Werner was standing there, or rather, he was sitting. The water was only a hand's breadth below the window and he was sitting in the boat that used to be in his yard, a little cockleshell made of moulded plastic, more like a child's boat, a toy, and he called, 'Get your things.' He wore a yellow plastic sou'wester over his head, the kind you find in the souvenir shops at the beach, stacked on the shelves next to painted seashells, ship-in-a-bottle kits and stripy jerseys. Two drops of water ran down from his eyes to his lined and wrinkled cheeks and the smooth patches under his eyes were dull, as though they had caught the damp.

'No,' Maren had said when I asked her whether he suspected anything. No. Meaning not that he didn't suspect but that I shouldn't ask. As she spoke she ran her finger over the burn marks between my shoulder blades. I was lying on my belly and as I turned over she began to breath heavily, that way she had, her ribs showing against the skin below her astonishingly large breasts. It was almost dark, late afternoon, feeding time in the barns, the sound of cattle stamping and lowing, and as she bent forward I saw her self-inflicted wounds, the scars on the inside of her legs where she cut at herself with a razor—red welts, beginning a hand's breadth down her thighs, each a centimetre below the one above, so that I suddenly thought that inflicting pain had something to do with precision, that as well as her knife she needed a tape measure to do it. 'Maren,' I said, but she had dropped her head, her hair hung down, covering her face, her fingers drew circles, larger and larger, on my ribcage, my belly, and stopped at last between my legs. And not twenty minutes later, I saw her walking through the gap in the fence, under the dripping trees, to her husband's farmyard. Every day, so that in the end, I began to look at the clock long before five.

'Hand over!' said Werner.

I passed the suitcase through the window, he stowed it under the bench and once I had squirmed through the hatch we paddled off through the garden, over the sunken village green. It had lost all semblance of its old round shape, only the roofs could still be seen, while the letterbox, the children's slide, the fire station, the extensions on the houses, the barns and the byres were almost entirely submerged. We paddled toward the street, higher up on the slope, where the villagers had taken refuge, those who had stayed behind, who hadn't left in their cars the day before. They stood about in little groups or sat on their suitcases bundled together under a tarpaulin in front of the substation and looked at the village, swallowed by the water, looked up at the old mine track where the bus was supposed to arrive.

Next to the substation, an asphalt path sloped down into the water. The heaps of potash had turned grey over the past few days, nearly dark grey, but couldn't be seen from the road as they lay behind a copse that likewise stuck out above the water. Far off, I could see the outlines of individual trees that showed where the ditches ran. The trees were reduced to the size of bushes now and the narrow ditches that caught the water in spring and autumn were vanished under more water than ever before. The rain dimpled the surface of water stretching as far as the mine track in the east, the hills behind the highway in the west, as far as the horizon to the north, lost in the haze. After the snow at the end of October, now it was mid-December and as warm as spring. If it hadn't been for the rain, we could have walked round in light pullovers, but as it was the villagers were wearing their waterproofs, yellow and blue, which made them look incongruously jolly, like beachcombers out for a day on the shore, who had suddenly been cast adrift here between the drowned village and the drowned fields, and only their round flat faces, marked by hard work or hard drinking or both, their look of worry and exhaustion showed that they hadn't gathered here for fun, that they weren't holidaymakers but refugees. Their timber-frame houses were painted with the words *Preserve us, O Lord, from the Fire*, but now the water had fallen from the heavens and risen from the caverns and the deep places of the earth to the surface.

Once we had pulled the boat up onto the road, Werner went to Maren, who was sitting on a folding chair that she had obviously brought along with her. She was wearing a black raincoat, drops of rain dripped from an umbrella in her hand and fell to the ground like strings of pearls, and she looked across. She looked at us, and when he put his hand on her shoulder, she took it and put it to her mouth, her lips parted. He stood behind her, not sheltered by the umbrella. The rain ran over his child's sou'wester and over his waterproof, then dripped down into his boots, too wide at the top, while she held his hand and covered it slowly with kisses, not taking her eyes off me, almost as she had that afternoon—except that then, she had been holding my hand and looking across at him.

She had come over around five, once again, and as she sat astride me, I inside her, she shoved me backwards by the shoulders with more strength than I would ever have believed her capable of—she was such a thin person—and sat up, ramrod straight. Her legs had been clamped round me like a vice but now parted, so that I saw the lines of scars that led up like two tiny ladders. Then she took my hand and began to kiss it slowly, absent-mindedly, while her eyes slid past me to the window. When I turned my head I saw that the kisses were not meant for me but for her husband, whose brow was pressed against the windowpane. He stood beneath the eaves and looked in, while she sat astride me and covered my fingers with fluttering kisses. 'Maren,' I whispered, 'Maren, no,' and at that she shifted her weight and pressed her pelvis against mine. Her eyes gazed at the window, while down below the sheath of muscle clenched and relaxed, seemingly of its own accord, holding the whole length of me, the shaft, a squeezing and rubbing deep inside, a kneading that made me forget all about him, until slowly I remembered. 'Maren,' I said again, 'Maren,' pushed her off me, turned round and saw that he was still standing there, or rather, that he stepped back as soon as our eyes met, and vanished into the dark.

The next day I kept the doors locked. She turned the handle but I shouted for her to go away, and when I went for my walk through the village that night, he followed me.

'Thomas,' he whispered, 'Thomas.' He walked beside me and whispered, 'If you'd like to unlock the doors again, Thomas.' His voice wheedled in my ear. But I walked on, faster and faster, leaving him behind at last. It was late October, the smell of snow in the air, and indeed as I turned onto the asphalt path the first flakes began to fall gently on me as tiny crystals of ice that clung to my hair, the stubble of my beard, the folds of my skin, my jacket, so that when I got back home at two o'clock, two in the morning, I looked like a snowman, and when I put my hand on the door handle I felt something hard that clattered against the wooden door. I put the light on and saw that it was the key, someone had tied it onto the door handle by its leather strip, the same key that had fallen out of her trouser pocket one day, large, iron, scaled with rust, a heavy thing that was more like a tool than a key, and when I picked it up she had shoved it hastily back into her pocket. I took it into the house with me, thinking I would hang it on her door the next morning, on their door, but then I felt nervous about going onto their property and it stayed in the hallway. For weeks it lay on the little table next to the wardrobe, sometimes my hand reached for it and then jerked back, until the night at the end of November when I grasped it after all.

Now we could see the lights of settlements near the motorway more and more often, looming up through the darkness, sometimes the lights of small villages, a few flickering lamps, sometimes towns which made the sky glow above them. As far as could be seen the floodwaters had spared the region we were driving through now, or the water had drained back into the caverns and caves as quickly as it had spilt out. Dry land, so there was no more need to truck us along the motorway with a promise of camp beds, warm soup and hot tea. But the man up there at the front, the man at the wheel, made no move to turn off the road at any of the signposts that patched the skin of the darkness, rather, he trundled along in the middle lane, and his curses had died away—which I had taken for impatience at not finding our destination, impatience with the road but with himself as well—he had stopped cursing and instead, was humming softly, a hum that blended in with the sound of the engine.

'Listen,' I said, 'Listen to me, that's enough.'

I had walked up behind him again and was looking over his shoulder into the brightness of the middle distance, pushed along in front of us by the headlights. A motorway bridge approached, with a bus standing on it and people who had climbed down from the bus. They were lined up in rows, standing at the railing, looking down, and as we drew near I could see (as much as I could see anything in that light) that they were dressed as though for a public event or a funeral, the men in black suits, the women in black dresses, and their faces were so white in the light of the headlamps that slid over them for a moment that I thought of those others, the dark-clad, stiff figures that had sailed past my window on a summer's day six months ago on the *Ace of Clubs*. And then we were through, under the bridge, and the driver had looked up as well, and I heard him say in his bubbling voice, 'Now.' (Or at least that's what I understood, Now.) Then he changed lanes, the bushes flew past so close to the right-hand windows that they seemed to brush against them, and when I went back to my seat I noticed that the villagers had woken up—the hunchbacked man with the head so small that it seemed you could close your two hands round it, the old woman who shuffled out of her house in clogs and bought sliced bread at the mobile shop that came once a week, the young woman with twins, who dressed in a brightly-coloured jogging suit and was so fat that she could only walk the streets with the greatest difficulty (a stranded marine mammal) and who now filled two seats on the left of the aisle, she and all the others I had never seen in the months I had spent in their community, since they never came out of their houses, the invisible ones, the ones left behind, finally washed out of their lairs and onto the road in front of the substation by the rising water, last of all Werner and Maren, that's to say, Werner was asleep while Maren's eyes were open. She sat there ramrod straight and though she usually let her hair fall loose, carelessly, now she had combed it fiercely back, as she had worn it the evening I saw her sitting in her room.

Yes, it was late November, I still kept the door locked but that didn't change the fact that I was already looking at the clock long before five o'clock, as though I wanted her visits to resume, the same every time as they had been. She would come through the garden, open the door (soon enough she stopped even knocking), take her boots off in the hall by putting the toe of one to the heel of the other, then would come into the room in her socks, the room where I sat watching her, first through the window and then from my desk, while she in turn hardly lifted her head, seeming to look at me without seeing, at best letting her eyes stop for a moment, mocking, on my neck, my shoulders, arms and legs. And the lovemaking? Sometimes, rarely, only exceptionally, it was a long-drawn-out affair, fingers feeling their way across skin and sketching circles, kissing of hands, but mostly, it was headlong, wordless, short, with her mouth so close to my ear that I could feel her breath but would hardly ever hear a sound except a desperate *ahh*, as though all the world's pain were concentrated in this *ahh*, bundled up into a three-letter word, as though the pain were breaking free from her, and when she raised her head, it was as though the pain were sealed away again inside. And then, at the end of November, when I had almost forgotten, it returned, as though it had been sleeping all these weeks and now had woken again, this word, this sound, with something sensuous about it now, *ahh*, when I got up in the morning and went into the kitchen, *ahh*, in the afternoon, as I sat at the desk and thought of all the people I had met, Daniel, Wilhelm, Konrad, Suse, Katharina, *ahh*, and at night as well, when I stood in the hallway and ran my hand over the rusty piece of iron, I could hear it, *ahh*, until I no longer knew whether perhaps I should not take up that invitation. My hand hung above the key and jerked back, but that night, as I stood there once more, dropped back down again—I took the key and put it in my pocket, not intending to use it but simply to have with me on my nightly walks along the asphalt paths.

The period of drizzle had ended and a pouring rain had begun, the water tipped down, flowed through the village, pooled in the meadows, and when I went out into the village that night I saw that the paths were unwalkable, that there was nothing left for me to do but turn round, back to the village. On my way out—about half past one, again—the village had lain in deep darkness but when I came back to the round village green I saw light behind Maren and Werner's window shutters and turned into their yard, toward the sound of the rain drumming on the corrugated iron roof over their porch.

The house stood with its gable end to the green, with the door at the side, a wooden door with three steps leading up to it and in front of those a little lake made by the pattering rain. Once I had climbed the steps, I fumbled for the lock, and when I found it I put in the key, turned it, pressed the handle down and went in, passing from the darkness outside into the deeper darkness inside the house. 'Maren,' I called, my voice low, 'Maren?' Nothing. The room where I had seen the light was upstairs, so I felt my way to the stairs, which had to be in front of me since all these houses were built more or less the same. Yes, that was the kitchen door to the left, with an indefinable smell coming through into the hallway, and a sort of wardrobe to the right or something for hanging clothes at any rate, and then up the stairs, holding on to the banister, and half way up I could see light above me. 'Maren,' I called again, quietly, more quietly than my footsteps, more quietly than the rain drumming on the iron roof, the rain I heard the whole time, quietly, in case it was her sitting there and not him, in case he was asleep, so that I would not wake him.

But they were both there, both awake, looking as though they had been to bed and then got up again, both in dressing gowns, his was red-and-blue striped, hers was white. She sat in a chair, he was standing, as though he had just come in through the other door, the door on the other side of the room, open so that I could see the end of the bed from where I stood looking through the door ajar on my side, the bed linen and then behind that, dimly, the wall. He stood by the door. She must have been up for a while now, since her hair was combed, pulled back severely instead of hanging loose in strands as it usually did, while his hair—thin, fair, tousled—was plastered to his head with sweat.

'Maren,' he said, 'Maren, come back to bed then.'

And he took one step forward into the light of the little lamps that hung on tracks round the ceiling, the smooth patches below his eyes were shot through with a tracery of tiny blood vessels which pulsed and ticked, seeming to tremble. Her hands were under her dressing gown, her legs crossed, one foot dangling free, and as the foot began to tremble, she raised her head and looked at Werner as though she wanted to say something, then uncrossed her legs, put her feet on the floor and looked up at the ceiling. 'Maren,' he said, 'I'm sorry, it's not you, you're wonderful, but I . . .' and he came toward her, knelt in front of her and buried his face in her lap. After a while her hand appeared, she took her hand out from under her dressing gown and stroked his hair, then her other hand came out and I could see that it held something. She put her arm out to her side and let it land by the chair and as she opened her hand, something fell to the floor—a little knife, its blade pointing toward the door where I stood peering into the room. He was still kneeling, while her eyes were fixed somewhere, perhaps above the window, some point in space I could not see from where I was. And when she put her other hand on Werner's head, I went downstairs, hung the key on one of the hooks in the wardrobe and went out into the yard.

Meanwhile, the bus had turned off the motorway, taking a long curve to the right, and was bumping along a country road. The lights of windmills showed between the bushes, in the same formation I had seen them from the asphalt paths, and just as I was beginning to believe that we had come back to the village, travelling a huge circle, the road became wider and we arrived in a town, a part of town that looked something like the towns I used to walk through at night after we had put in to dock. Streetlamps casting red light down on a crossroads, filling stations, blocks of flats in a row, a metal gate rolled down in an entranceway. But when we came to the middle of town, we seemed to be driving through a film set for a costume drama—timber-framed houses, bow windows, the brass plates hanging on chains in front of the shops showing the old guild symbols of each trade, as though we had found our way into some vast pedestrian precinct, a medieval town polished till it shone. Was this where the driver was supposed to bring us? The tugging, tearing feeling was back, threatening to pull me apart and all at once, I knew that I wanted to go back, back to the rivers, the docks, the warehouses where a man could lose himself walking round, not back to my flat by the river but to a boat, and what if my licence had expired, I'd just start again from the beginning.

The driver bent low over the wheel, his head cocked to one side as though he were trying to make out a street name, turned off and then stopped on a square where little wooden cabins had been set up. Garlands of pine branches overhung the paths between the cabins, studded with electric candles. He stopped, and when I looked out, I saw that we had drawn up next to another bus that stood pointing the other way at the side of the road, so that its front door was about level with our back door. It was a large touring bus with black windows, so that I could see no one behind the panes, nothing, not the least detail. It stood there as though empty, parked up and forgotten, but it was not empty. I believed (and I still believe today) that the people who sat in the bus were the same who had watched us coming from the motorway bridge.

When I asked the driver later what kind of bus that was, he shrugged his shoulders. As he drew up, he opened the door. Maren and Werner had already gone up the aisle and they slipped out, then got into the other bus straightaway, through the rear door, which had opened like a black maw. Maren went first, Werner following, and as he put his foot on the lowest step he turned round one last time and looked back, and although it was dark, the light coming from our headlamps lit the passage between the two buses a little, and I saw those patches under his eyes again, the gleaming patches where fear had gathered.

Maren had already got in but he was still standing there, looking backwards, uncertain whether he should follow her, and suddenly I felt sorry that we had never spoken more than those words at the fence, in the village when he followed me down the street (and on that occasion I hadn't spoken at all, he was the one who spoke) and then in the toy boat. He hesitated a moment longer, then squared his shoulders, climbed aboard, the door shut behind him straightaway and the bus glided off.

The rest, ah well, the rest is quickly told. Yes, this was the town where the emergency accommodation had been set up. There was hot tea, soup, wool blankets, friendly words and a television set switched on in the corner, where I saw the Federal Chancellor, wearing an army jacket, standing atop a wall of sandbags, a shovel in his hand as though he and he alone had built the wall against the flood, and he made a speech using the word *Dezemberflut*, which was picked up by the press. The December flood. Or was it the other way round? Had he picked up the word from the press? *Dezemberflut*, it said in the newspapers I bought next morning at the railway station. I read them on the train and looked out of the window, where the fields glided past, blanketed with hoarfrost after the temperature had plunged during the night.